Journey Beyond

by

Anna Regala

ISBN: 979-8-3291-5312-5

Published by: Anna Regala

To my dad in heaven,

For all the love and sacrifices you made for me and our family. I hope you are proud of me and smiling up there.

Prologue

In the quiet, sun-soaked streets of a small town in the Philippines, a woman named Maria often found herself gazing up at the sky, imagining the vast world beyond her island. At 27 years old, Maria had spent most of her life in this town, rich in tradition and community, which felt like a cocoon—comfortable yet confining. Growing up in a middle-class family, she lived contentedly, but dreams of traveling overseas seemed like distant stars, visible yet unattainable.

As a child, Maria would sit by the window of her modest home, listening to the hum of daily life around her. The laughter of children playing in the streets, the distant calls of street vendors, and the gentle rustling of the palm trees created a symphony that was both familiar and comforting. Yet beyond this comforting cocoon, she dreamed of distant lands, of cultures and experiences far removed from her own.

Maria's parents, hardworking and ever supportive, instilled in her the values of perseverance and hope. They encouraged her curiosity and nurtured her dreams, even when the path ahead seemed unclear. "Education is your key to a better future," they often said, and she clung to this belief with all her heart.

Through the years, Maria faced numerous challenges and setbacks. There were times when her dreams felt impossibly far away, obscured by the harsh realities of life. Yet, each obstacle became a stepping stone, each setback a lesson. She learned the power of resilience, the importance of staying true to her dreams, and the value of unwavering determination.

In these moments of struggle and uncertainty, Maria's faith in God was her anchor. She found solace and strength in prayer, trusting that He had a plan for her, even when the path seemed obscure. Her faith guided her through the darkest times and illuminated her way forward, providing a source of unwavering hope and inspiration.

Now, at 39, as Maria looks back on her journey, she is filled with gratitude and awe. The woman who once dreamed by the window has traveled the world, experienced cultures beyond her wildest imaginings, and built a life that transcends her humble beginnings. This book is a testament to that journey—a story of dreams realized, of battles fought and won, and of the relentless pursuit of a life beyond the ordinary.

Through these pages, Maria hopes to inspire others to dream boldly, to face challenges head-on, and to never lose sight of the stars they reach for. Because if a young woman from a small town in the Philippines can find her place in the world, so can anyone.

Chapter 1: A Heart Full of Dreams

As the final bell rings, signaling the end of the school year, Maria Rodriguez stands at the front of her classroom. Her voice carries a mix of warmth and finality as she calls out, "Goodbye and thank you, class!"

In unison, the students respond, "Goodbye and thank you, Ms. Rodriguez."

She watches them gather their belongings and file out of the room, their laughter and chatter echoing down the hallway. As the last student leaves, a quiet hush settles over the classroom, a silence that feels both liberating and bittersweet. Maria feels a pang of nostalgia mixed with a deep sense of satisfaction, knowing that today, her students have walked away with new knowledge and experiences.

In her seven years of teaching at St. Michael's Catholic School, Maria has experienced countless moments of joy, frustration, and personal growth. Each year, she has witnessed the transformation of eager minds, nurturing their curiosity and guiding them toward understanding. It has been a privilege to be part of their journey, to witness the spark of discovery in their eyes as they grasp new concepts or overcome challenges.

As she begins tidying up the classroom, a group of her students lingers at the door, hesitant to leave.

"Ms. Rodriguez," a boy named Leo calls out, "are you going to teach us next year too?"

Maria smiles warmly. "I don't know, Leo. We'll have to see what the future holds. But wherever I am, I know you'll all do great things."

"Do you ever get tired of teaching us?" a girl named Sarah asks, her eyes wide with curiosity.

"Never," Maria replies with a gentle laugh. "Teaching you all has been one of the most rewarding things I've ever done. Each of you brings something special to this classroom."

"But Ms. Rodriguez," chimes in another student, Mark, "if you could do anything else, what would it be?"

Maria pauses, considering the question. "Well, Mark, sometimes I dream about exploring different paths. Maybe being a lawyer, a doctor, or even a psychologist. There are so many possibilities out there."

"Really?" Sarah's eyes light up. "But you're such a great teacher. Why would you want to do something else?"

"It's not about wanting to leave teaching," Maria explains thoughtfully. "It's about being curious and open to new experiences. Just like how I encourage all of you to explore and learn, I want to do the same for myself."

"Do you think you'll ever leave us, Ms. Rodriguez?" Alvin's voice holds a hint of sadness.

"Change is a part of life," Maria says gently. "But just because I might explore something new doesn't mean I'll forget about you. You'll always be a special part of my journey."

The students nod, absorbing her words, before finally heading out the door. Maria watches them go, feeling a mixture of pride and longing. The chalk dust, the rows of desks, and the daily lessons—while comforting and rewarding, sometimes feel like a box she needs to step out of.

She often finds herself dreaming about other paths. What would it be like to argue a case in court as a lawyer, to diagnose and heal as a doctor, to explore the human mind as a psychologist? Or to try something completely different, to see what else the world has to offer beyond teaching?

This desire for new experiences nags at her, a constant reminder that there's a whole world out there waiting to be explored. It's not that she's unhappy with teaching—she loves it deeply—but there's a part of her that's curious about what else she could do. She wants to push her boundaries and see where new paths might lead.

Standing in the quiet, empty classroom, Maria realizes that while this chapter of her life has been fulfilling, it's just the beginning. There are new adventures out there, new dreams to chase, and she's ready to embrace them, heart and soul.

As she turns off the lights and closes the door behind her, Maria feels a sense of anticipation. The future is wide open, and she's ready to explore whatever comes next.

Chapter 2: New Horizons

"Maria, I heard from Joy that her dad's boss is hiring Filipinos to manage their supermarkers in Papua New Guinea! I'm interested. I'm going to the interview at the mall this afternoon. Do you want to come with me too?" Christine's eyes sparkled with excitement as she shared the news. They were in the teachers' lounge, unwinding after the last class of the day. Christine, a good friend and colleague, always had a knack for bringing a burst of energy into the room.

Joy, a common sophomore student of theirs, had eagerly passed along this opportunity. As Christine spoke, a surge of anticipation stirred within Maria, tinged with a touch of disbelief. The prospect of her dream of traveling becoming a reality felt surreal, yet deeply exhilarating. She had always yearned to explore new places, but this was the first time such a tangible opportunity had presented itself.

"Papua New Guinea?" Maria repeated, almost to herself. "That sounds... amazing."

Christine nodded enthusiastically. "Yes! Imagine the adventure, Maria. A whole new culture, new experiences... and it's a great chance to advance our careers."

Despite the initial rush of excitement, questions began to surface in Maria's mind, causing a ripple of uncertainty amidst her burgeoning enthusiasm.

"What about our students?" Maria mused aloud, thinking about the young faces she had grown to cherish over the years. While she had expressed her love for teaching, she also knew that she wasn't bound to stay forever. "How would they react if I left?"

Christine placed a reassuring hand on Maria's shoulder. "You've given them so much already, Maria. They would understand if you chose to explore a new path. They know you care about them, and they'll be okay."

Maria nodded slowly, appreciating Christine's words. "And what about Jeff? How do I even begin to tell him? We've talked about our future together here."

"You'll need to talk it through with him," Christine advised gently. "If he truly cares for you, he'll understand your need to explore and grow."

Maria sighed, the weight of these conversations looming large in her mind. And then there was her family. They had always been her rock, their love and guidance shaping her journey thus far. How would they react to the news of her potentially moving to a distant land?

"I guess there's only one way to find out," Maria said with a mix of determination and apprehension. "Let's go to the interview."

Later that afternoon, Maria and Christine found themselves at the mall, ready to face the interview with a blend of hope and trepidation. They stepped into the coffee shop where they were greeted by Joy's father, Mr. Dela Cruz. His warm and genial presence was immediately reassuring.

"Christine, Maria, it's good to see you both," Mr. Dela Cruz greeted them with a broad smile. "I'm really glad you're considering this opportunity. Pete, my boss, is eager to meet you."

He led them to a corner table where Pete, an Australian gentleman with a calm demeanor and friendly disposition, was waiting. His casual but professional attire contrasted with the usual formality they were used to in such meetings, which put them at ease.

"Good day, Christine, Maria. I'm Pete. It's great to meet you both," he said, extending a hand. His accent and relaxed tone instantly made Maria feel more comfortable.

"Nice to meet you, Pete," Christine responded with a confident smile. "We're really interested in learning more about the opportunity."

"Absolutely," Maria added, trying to keep her voice steady despite the flutter of nerves.

Pete smiled warmly. "I'm glad to hear that. We're looking for motivated individuals who are eager to bring their skills and enthusiasm to our team in Papua New Guinea. It's a vibrant place, full of opportunities and challenges."

The interview progressed smoothly. Pete asked about their teaching experience, their ability to manage teams, and their adaptability to new environments. Throughout the conversation, Maria felt a growing sense of determination. This could be her chance to explore new horizons, to experience life abroad, and to support her family in ways she had never imagined.

After a thorough discussion, Pete leaned back in his chair and nodded thoughtfully. "You both seem like a great fit for what we're looking for," he said with a genuine smile. "Congratulations! You are hired!"

Christine let out a small gasp of joy, and Maria felt a rush of exhilaration wash over her. This was it—the opportunity she had dreamed of.

"Thank you so much!" Maria said, her voice filled with gratitude and excitement.

"Thank you, Pete!" Christine echoed, her eyes gleaming with anticipation.

As they left the mall, the reality of their decision began to sink in. They were stepping into a new chapter of their lives, one that promised adventure and growth.

"Can you believe it, Maria? We're going to Papua New Guinea!" Christine's voice was brimming with excitement.

"It feels like a dream," Maria replied, still processing the whirlwind of the afternoon. "But there's a lot to think about... my family, Jeff, the students."

"We'll figure it out," Christine said, linking her arm with Maria's. "This is a huge step, but it's also a chance for us to grow and experience something completely new. We've got each other, and we'll make it work."

Maria nodded, feeling a blend of hope and trepidation. As they walked through the bustling mall, she realized that this decision was just the beginning. There would be challenges ahead, but for now, she was ready to embrace whatever the future held.

Chapter 3: Dreams and Doubts

Maria sat at the kitchen table, her parents' faces reflecting a mix of concern and disbelief. They had always been her biggest supporters, but the news she was about to share felt like a storm brewing on the horizon.

"Abroad? Papua New Guinea?" Her father's voice rose in pitch, incredulous. "Are you serious, Maria? What will you do there? You don't even hold a managerial degree. Who told you about this? Do you really believe them?"

Her mother's worry was palpable. "Why so far away? And in a job that's not even related to your teaching career. How can you be sure this is safe?"

Maria took a deep breath, trying to steady her voice. "Christine and I went to the interview. Pete, the owner, seemed genuine, and he offered us both positions. This is a real opportunity, Mama, Papa. A chance to experience something new and grow."

"But this isn't like moving to Manila or Cebu," her father insisted. "This is a different country altogether, so far from home."

"I know, Papa. And it scares me too. But I've always wanted to see the world, to explore. This could be my chance."

Her mother's eyes softened, but the worry remained. "We've always supported you, Maria. But you're talking about moving thousands of miles away. How will you manage without us?"

Maria felt a lump in her throat. "I'm not asking for permission. I'm telling you because I need your support. I'm scared too, but I feel like I need to do this. For me."

The room fell silent, the weight of her words hanging in the air. Maria could see the struggle in her parents' eyes, torn between their desire to protect her and their wish to see her spread her wings.

That night, in the quiet sanctuary of her room, Maria knelt beside her bed and prayed. "Dear God, whatever Your will, please guide me. Help me find the strength to follow my dreams, even when it's hard."

She sat back on her heels, feeling a sense of calm wash over her. She knew the path ahead wouldn't be easy, but she trusted that she was being guided towards something greater.

Later, she picked up her phone and dialed Jeff's number. He was away at a conference, but they had always been open with each other. She hoped he would understand, even if it meant a big change in their plans.

"Hey, Jeff," she began hesitantly when he answered. "I need to talk to you about something important."

"Hey, Maria. What's up?" His voice was warm, but she could sense the underlying tiredness from his long day.

"I got a job offer. In Papua New Guinea."

There was a brief silence. "Papua New Guinea? That's... really far, Maria. What kind of job?"

"I'd be managing supermarkets. It's a big step, but it's also an amazing opportunity. I know it's not what we planned, but I really want to take this chance."

Jeff's tone shifted, his voice becoming more serious. "And what about us? What about our plans? This isn't just about a job; it's about our future together."

"I know," Maria replied softly. "But I think this could be a way for us to grow, too. Maybe you could find something there, and we could still be together."

Jeff sighed deeply. "I don't think it's that simple, Maria. This changes everything. I need time to think."

"Of course," Maria said, her heart sinking. "Take all the time you need."

As the call ended, Maria felt a heavy sense of uncertainty. She had expected resistance, but she hadn't anticipated how deeply it would affect her.

The next morning, Maria sat with Chu, the school's bookkeeper and a trusted friend. They had found a quiet corner in the teachers' lounge to talk.

"Chu, I have some big news," Maria began, her voice trembling slightly. "I've been offered a job... and it's abroad."

Chu's eyes widened, her face breaking into a warm smile. "Maria, that's amazing! I knew you could do it. Tell me everything."

Maria took a deep breath and recounted the interview with Pete, the unexpected job offer, and the excitement she felt. "It's in Papua New Guinea. I'd be managing supermarkets. It's a huge step, and a little scary, but it feels like a dream come true."

Chu listened intently, her expression thoughtful. "It's a big step, Maria. It's natural for your parents to be worried. They've always seen you as their little girl, close to home. But you have to follow your heart. This is your dream, and you have the right to pursue it."

"I know, but what if I'm making a mistake? What if I lose everything I care about because of this?"

Chu reached across the table and took Maria's hand. "You're 27, Maria. You have your whole life ahead of you. Yes, your plans with Jeff might get delayed, and this decision might affect your relationship. But if he truly loves you, he'll find a way to support you. And as for your family, they love you deeply. They'll come around."

Maria looked down at their joined hands, a mix of relief and doubt washing over her. "I hope you're right," she said, her voice barely above a whisper. "I've never felt so torn."

Chu smiled gently. "You're stronger than you think, Maria. And sometimes, the most important dreams require the biggest risks."

Taking a deep breath, Maria shared her concerns about Jeff. "Jeff didn't take the news well. He said he needed time to think, but I don't know if he'll ever really be okay with this."

"Have faith in your relationship," Chu advised. "But also be prepared for the possibility that he might not see things the same way. This is a chance for you to grow, Maria. And you have to trust that everything will work out as it's meant to."

Maria nodded, feeling a glimmer of hope. "Thank you, Chu. I don't know what I'd do without your support."

Days turned into a week, and during that time, Maria's parents slowly began to come to terms with her decision. One morning, as they sat down for breakfast, her father broke the silence.

"When do you plan to complete the requirements for your visa?" he asked, his tone surprisingly calm.

Maria looked up, startled. "I'm still gathering everything. I wasn't sure when to start because I didn't want to push you."

Her mother added, "We'll help you get everything sorted. I'll talk to your Aunt Luisa about borrowing some money for your allowance."

Maria's eyes filled with tears of relief and gratitude. "Thank you, Mama, Papa. This means so much to me."

Her father nodded, his expression softening. "We may not fully understand why you want to go so far away, but we trust you. Just promise you'll stay safe and keep in touch."

"I will," Maria assured them, her heart swelling with love and appreciation.

That evening, Maria called Jeff again, bracing herself for the conversation they needed to have.

"Hey, Jeff. Can we talk about Papua New Guinea?" she asked, her voice steady but apprehensive.

Jeff sighed on the other end of the line. "Maria, I've been thinking a lot about this. I don't think I can do it. The distance, the uncertainty... it's too much."

"Jeff, I understand it's a lot to take in. But I really believe this is a great opportunity for us to grow, both individually and together. Maybe we can find a way to make it work?"

There was a long pause. Then, Jeff's voice came through, colder than before. "Maria, I don't think we want the same things anymore. I can't support this decision. I'm breaking up with you."

Maria's heart shattered. "Jeff, please, let's talk about this. We've been through so much together."

"I'm sorry, Maria. I can't do this," Jeff said, and the line went dead.

Maria sat in stunned silence, the weight of his words sinking in. Tears filled her eyes as she whispered to the empty room, "God, please guide me. I don't know if I can do this alone."

But as the tears fell, she felt a spark of resolve deep within her. She knew the path she had chosen was not going to be easy, but it was hers to walk. And despite the fear and the heartache, she was ready to face whatever lay ahead.

As the sun rose the next morning, Maria stood by her window, looking out at the world beyond. She felt a sense of quiet determination. The journey to Papua New Guinea was just beginning, and though the road was uncertain, she knew she had the strength to navigate it.

Maria made her way to the school, her resignation letter tucked securely in her bag. She knew that this conversation would mark the end of a chapter in her life, but it was also the first step toward a new beginning.

Entering the principal's office, Maria took a deep breath and delivered her resignation letter. The principal, though saddened by Maria's departure, understood her desire for new challenges and opportunities. They shared a heartfelt conversation, reminiscing about Maria's years of service and the impact she had made on the school community.

As Maria packed up her belongings and said her farewells to her colleagues and students, she couldn't help but feel a twinge of sadness mingled with excitement. Leaving behind the familiar comforts of her teaching job was bittersweet, but she knew that greater adventures awaited her on the horizon.

With her resignation finalized, Maria returned home, her heart heavy yet hopeful. With her family's support finally behind her and a new horizon awaiting, she took a deep breath and prepared to step into the unknown, trusting that this leap of faith would lead her to the life she had always dreamed of.

Chapter 4: Crossroads of Challenges and Opportunities

The cabin of the plane hummed softly as Maria stared out the window, her heart heavy with a mix of sadness and excitement. The past few days had been a whirlwind of emotions, culminating in a tearful farewell with Jeff and a bittersweet goodbye to her family. She had thought she was one hundred percent ready for this new chapter in her life, but as the plane soared through the clouds toward Papua New Guinea, she realized that she wasn't as prepared as she had believed.

Maria's thoughts were interrupted by the sound of voices nearby. Turning slightly in her seat, she saw Rey and Teresa, her fellow travelers on this journey to a new land. Rey, a former expat in Papua New Guinea, seemed to exude a sense of world-weariness as he shared stories of his time in the country.

"Papua New Guinea isn't quite the paradise Pete described it to be," Rey remarked, his tone tinged with a hint of cynicism. "Sure, it has its beauty, but it's also a place of challenges and uncertainties."

Teresa nodded in agreement, her expression solemn. "I've heard about the security concerns there. It must be difficult for expats to adjust."

Maria listened intently, her heart sinking with each cautionary tale. She had been so focused on the promise of adventure and opportunity that she hadn't fully considered the potential risks and hardships of life in Papua New Guinea.

As Rey continued to recount his experiences with rascals and the need for tight security measures, Maria felt a pang of anxiety gnawing at her. What had she gotten herself into? Was she truly ready for the realities of living in a foreign land, far from the comforts of home?

But amid the uncertainty and doubt, Maria clung to a flicker of hope. She reminded herself of the reasons why she had embarked on this journey—the chance to explore new horizons, to challenge herself, and to make a difference in the lives of others. Despite the challenges ahead, she was determined to embrace this opportunity with courage and resilience.

As the plane continued its journey toward their destination, Maria closed her eyes and whispered a silent prayer for strength and guidance. She knew that the road ahead would be filled with obstacles and hardships, but she also believed that it held the promise of growth, discovery, and new beginnings.

With a renewed sense of resolve, Maria leaned back in her seat and allowed herself to envision the possibilities that lay beyond the horizon. Though her heart may be heavy with the weight of farewells and uncertainty, she was ready to embark on this journey of heartbreak and hope, trusting that it would lead her to a place of fulfillment and purpose.

Upon arrival, Maria, Rey, and Teresa were greeted by Edgar, a friendly Filipino man who served as one of the security managers. "Welcome to Popondetta," Edgar said warmly, offering a reassuring smile as he guided them toward their destination.

Edgar shared stories about the rascals and thieves that were known to frequent the area, heightening Maria's sense of apprehension. Finally, they reached their destination—a sprawling compound consisting of expat accommodation and several supermarkets.

Inside the office, Noel, the accountant, Pete, and Mr. Dela Cruz, whose name was Alfred, greeted them warmly. "Welcome, Maria, Rey, and Teresa," Noel said with a warm smile, extending a handshake to each of them. "We're thrilled to have you join our team. Before we get started, let me give you a quick orientation."

As Noel went over the details of their roles and responsibilities, Maria's excitement began to overshadow her initial apprehension. Surprisingly, they were informed that they would be receiving their two months' salary in advance.

Maria's eyes widened in disbelief. "Two months' salary in advance?" she exclaimed, her voice filled with astonishment. She had never heard of a company that was so generous, and the gesture filled her with gratitude and disbelief.

Maria wasted no time in phoning her mother and asking Noel to help her send the money to the Philippines. With all debts paid off on day one, Maria felt a sense of optimism and determination wash over her, ready to embrace the challenges and opportunities that lay ahead in this new chapter of her life.

Chapter 5: Settling into the Routine

Maria sat at her desk in the small, bustling office of the supermarket, balancing the sales ledger and calculating the daily totals. The rhythmic hum of activity filled the air, a comforting background to her focused work. She glanced at the clock; it was nearly time for the afternoon inventory with Rey and Teresa.

"I can't believe it's been a month already," Maria murmured to herself, shaking her head in disbelief. Time had flown by since she first set foot in Papua New Guinea. She had grown accustomed to the daily rhythm of life here, the routines that structured her days and gave them a sense of purpose.

As the office door swung open, Rey and Teresa walked in, ready for the stocktake. Rey had become a good friend and guide sharing his knowledge and experiences with Maria. Teresa, with her easygoing demeanor, had been a steady source of support.

"Ready for the inventory check?" Rey asked, a playful glint in his eye. "Hope you're up for the challenge, Maria. We have a lot to count today."

Maria smiled, closing her ledger. "Always ready. How are we looking today?"

"Pretty good," Teresa replied, checking her list. "But we need to keep an eye on the rice and sugar. They're flying off the shelves faster than we expected."

They moved through the aisles, methodically counting and recording the stock. As they worked, Maria found herself reflecting on how far she had come.

"It feels like we've settled into a good routine," she said, jotting down numbers. "I've even memorized the national anthem, '*Arise, All You Sons*,' for the Monday flag ceremonies. Who would've thought?"

Teresa laughed. "You've really adapted quickly, Maria. It's impressive."

"Yeah," Rey agreed, scanning the shelves. "It took me a lot longer to get used to the daily routines when I first came here. But you seem to be handling it all really well."

Maria nodded, thinking about her mornings. She'd wake up at 6 AM, savor a cup of coffee, and be at the supermarket before its 7 AM opening. Her days were filled with a myriad of tasks: overseeing office operations, making price tags, monitoring sales and price changes, and stepping in for inventory checks whenever a manager was out. The afternoons were often spent balancing the cash against the sales and preparing the payroll every fortnight.

She laughed softly. "It's a lot to juggle, but I'm getting the hang of it. And I'm learning something new every day."

Their conversation shifted to the supermarket's tight security measures, a necessary response to the frequent attempts at theft. Maria recalled some of the more surprising incidents she had witnessed.

"Can you believe someone tried to steal a whole chicken by hiding it under their skirt?" she recounted, shaking her head in amazement. "People get really creative with their methods."

Rey chuckled. "You'd be surprised. Security has to be on their toes all the time. Some customers are real pros at sneaking things out."

Teresa nodded. "We can't let our guard down for a second. It's a constant game of cat and mouse."

Their discussion reminded Maria of Edgar, the security manager who had welcomed them on their first day. He had a knack for making even the most serious situations light-hearted. She recalled the time he had played a joke on her involving *buai*, the betel nut that was a traditional chew in Papua New Guinea.

"Do you remember the time Edgar tricked me into eating *buai*?" Maria asked, grinning at the memory. "He said it was part of the local customs and that refusing would offend everyone."

Rey laughed, shaking his head. "Oh, I heard about that. How did it go?"

Maria rolled her eyes, her smile widening. "I tried my best to eat it, but it didn't quite suit my taste. Everyone had a good laugh at my expense."

Teresa chuckled. "*Buai* is definitely an acquired taste. Don't worry, you're not the only one who's been tricked into trying it."

Maria continued, "It was hilarious and a bit mortifying. Edgar had a good laugh and said, 'Welcome to the club, Maria!' I guess it's all part of the experience."

As they wrapped up their inventory, Maria couldn't help but feel a deep sense of gratitude for the friends she had made and the experiences she had encountered. The supermarket might have its challenges, but it was also a place of camaraderie and shared stories.

With the inventory done, they returned to the office. Maria finished balancing the day's sales and felt a sense of accomplishment wash over her. It wasn't just about the numbers; it was about the journey she was on, the people she was with, and the new life she was building.

Later, as they gathered in the staff clubhouse for dinner, Maria reflected on her day. The managers had their own cook, a small luxury that made the evenings more relaxing. Over the meal, they shared stories and laughter, reinforcing the bonds that had formed among them.

In quieter moments, Maria would think about home and the life she had left behind. But the routines and friendships here made the distance feel a little less daunting. She was finding her place in this new world, one day at a time.

Chapter 6: A New Arrival and an Unexpected Encounter

Two months had passed since Maria and Teresa had started their new roles at the supermarket. The daily grind was filled with challenges and small victories, yet an undercurrent of anticipation flowed as they awaited Christine's arrival. Her delayed visa had kept her away longer than expected, but today, their wait was finally over.

Maria stood at the entrance of the supermarket, her eyes scanning the surroundings. Edgar, a trusted colleague and driver, had offered to pick Christine up from the airport. When Maria saw Edgar's familiar car pull up, her heart leaped with joy. The car door opened, and Christine stepped out, her face lighting up with a radiant smile.

"Christine!" Maria rushed forward, her voice filled with excitement.

"Maria!" Christine replied, embracing her friend tightly. "It's so good to see you."

As they broke the embrace, Christine gestured to the tall, handsome man who had accompanied her. "Maria, this is Dean.

He's the co-manager at our other supermarket and just returned from a two-month vacation."

Dean extended his hand with a friendly smile. He was strikingly good-looking, with an athletic build and warm dark brown eyes that made Maria's pulse quicken.

"Nice to meet you, Maria," Dean said, his voice deep and pleasant.

Maria shook his hand, and immediately, she felt a jolt of electricity—a sensation she hadn't experienced since she first met Jeff. It caught her off guard, her heart skipping a beat. She quickly pulled her hand back, forcing a polite smile.

"Nice to meet you too, Dean. Welcome back."

As they walked towards the supermarket, Maria noticed the easy rapport between Christine and Dean. Their laughter and light conversation filled the air, and despite herself, Maria felt a pang of envy. Dean's presence reminded her too much of Jeff, stirring up emotions she wasn't ready to confront. She resolved to keep her distance from him.

Over the next few days, Christine settled into her role quickly. Although she was primarily assigned as the office manager at the other supermarket, she spent some time at Maria's location, helping with various tasks. Christine had a knack for making the best of any situation, and her culinary skills were a godsend. Maria and Teresa, who barely knew their way around a kitchen, were grateful for Christine's guidance.

"Let me show you how to make a proper lunch," Christine said one day, rolling up her sleeves. "We can't live off the free dinners from the clubhouse alone."

She took charge, guiding Maria and Teresa through the process of preparing a simple yet delicious meal. The kitchen was soon filled with the aroma of fresh ingredients and the sound of their laughter.

"Christine, you're a lifesaver,' Teresa said, sampling a spoonful of the dish they were preparing.

"Just happy to help," Christine replied with a smile, stirring the pot with practiced ease.

A week later, a significant change came to the team. Rey, who had been a cornerstone of their supermarket, was reassigned to the other location, where Christine would be managing the office. His departure left a noticeable gap, but there was a sense of optimism about the new dynamic. Maria knew they would manage, but she missed Rey's steady presence.

One morning, as Maria walked into the office, she was startled to see Dean sitting at Alfred's desk, deep in conversation with him. She paused at the door, unsure of what was happening.

"Maria, come in," Alfred called, waving her over. "We have some news."

Dean stood up, his expression serious yet friendly. "Maria, Alfred has assigned me as the new overall manager of this supermarket, so I'll be working with you from now on."

Maria's heart skipped a beat. The news hit her like a ton of bricks. She had been carefully avoiding Dean, and now he was to be her direct superior. She forced a smile, trying to hide her surprise.

"Oh, I see," she said, attempting to sound nonchalant. "Welcome aboard, Dean."

"Thanks, Maria. I'm looking forward to working together," Dean replied, extending his hand once more.

This time, Maria hesitated before shaking it, feeling that same unsettling spark. She quickly withdrew her hand and nodded, determined to keep their interactions as brief and professional as possible.

As Dean and Alfred continued their discussion, Maria slipped out of the office, her mind racing. With Rey gone and Dean stepping into the role, everything was shifting. She couldn't shake the feeling that her carefully constructed world was about to change, and she wasn't sure she was ready for it.

Chapter 7: New Challenges and Unavoidable Encounters

Maria sat at her small desk in the break room, her phone propped up against a coffee cup for her regular video call with her family back in the Philippines. The familiar faces of her parents and siblings filled the screen, bringing a smile to her face.

"Hi, *Ate*!" her younger sister, Lucy, greeted her cheerfully. "How's everything in Papua New Guinea?"

"Hi, everyone! I miss you all so much," Maria responded warmly. "Things are busy here, but I'm doing okay. How are you all?"

"We're doing well, *anak*. We miss you too," her mother said, her voice filled with love and warmth. "How's work? Are you getting along with your new colleagues?"

Maria nodded, keeping her smile in place. "Work is good. I'm learning a lot and meeting some great people."

Her father leaned closer to the camera, a concerned but patient look on his face. "Are you managing fine over there, Maria? We know it's not easy being so far from home."

Maria felt a pang of worry but kept it hidden behind her smile. "I'm doing fine, Papa. Just focusing on doing my best every day."

"We're proud of you, *anak*. Just keep taking care of yourself," her mother added with a reassuring smile.

Maria felt a wave of relief and gratitude. "Thanks, Mama. I'm aiming for that performance bonus that Pete gives out every two months. I'm hoping to get it one of these days, but it usually goes to the senior managers."

"Just keep pushing, *Ate*," Lucy chimed in. "You'll get it. We believe in you."

Maria's heart swelled with love. "Thanks, everyone. I'll keep trying my best."

After the call ended, Maria sat quietly, reflecting on her family's unwavering support. Despite her own worries about the lower exchange rate of the PNG Kina to the Philippine Peso, which had dropped from 21 to 14, she kept those concerns to herself. Her focus was on working hard and aiming for that elusive bonus to support her family better.

Determined to overcome the financial strain, Maria threw herself into her work with renewed vigor. She aimed to excel in every aspect of her job, though the coveted performance bonus remained elusive, typically awarded to the senior managers.

In her interactions with Dean, Maria maintained a strictly professional demeanor. They exchanged cordial greetings and kept their conversations focused on work. It wasn't easy for Maria to suppress the initial spark she felt around him, but she was determined to keep things strictly business.

One morning, everything changed when Teresa came down with the flu. Maria found herself standing in front of Alfred's desk, feeling a mix of apprehension and responsibility.

"Maria, with Teresa sick, we need you to step in and help Dean with the retail operations," Alfred said, his tone firm yet supportive. "Can you handle that?"

Maria felt her heart race. This was precisely the kind of interaction she had been trying to avoid. But she nodded, accepting the inevitable. "Of course. I'll do my best."

Later that day, Maria met Dean in the bustling supermarket aisles. He was busy checking the inventory and preparing for the upcoming stocktake.

"Hi, Maria," Dean greeted her with a warm smile. "Ready to dive into some retail operations?"

Maria nodded, trying to mask her nervousness. "Yes, Dean. Let's get started."

Dean began by explaining the more intricate details of the retail operations, areas she hadn't focused on deeply before. Although Maria had participated in stocktakes with Rey and Teresa in the past, she realized there was a lot more to learn about the complexities and finer points of managing inventory and operations efficiently.

"You've done stocktakes before, right?" Dean asked, as they stood in front of a display of canned goods.

"Yes, but not as detailed as this," Maria admitted. "Rey and Teresa usually handled most of it."

Dean nodded understandingly. "It can be a lot to manage, but once you get the hang of it, it's pretty straightforward. Let's start with how we handle inventory discrepancies."

He walked Maria through the steps, from identifying stock inconsistencies to resolving them. His explanations were clear and methodical, making the process seem less daunting.

"Here's how we track our inventory in detail," Dean said, guiding her through the system. "It's crucial to ensure we always have the right stock on hand without overordering."

Maria followed along, her initial apprehension slowly melting away. "I see. So it's about balancing availability and cost-efficiency."

"Exactly," Dean replied, clearly impressed by her quick grasp. "You're catching on fast."

As they worked together over the next few days, Maria began to feel more at ease. Dean was knowledgeable and approachable, his teaching style making complex tasks easier to understand. Gradually, Maria found herself enjoying their interactions.

One afternoon, while they were organizing a particularly challenging section of the stockroom, Dean looked over at Maria with a smile. "You're doing great, Maria. You've got a real knack for this."

"Thank you, Dean," Maria replied, a genuine smile spreading across her face. "I'm learning a lot. It's not as intimidating as I thought."

Dean's eyes softened. "I'm glad to hear that. And remember, if you ever have questions or need help, I'm here."

Maria nodded, feeling a warmth spread through her. "I appreciate that, Dean. Really."

As they continued working, Maria realized that her initial apprehensions had been misplaced. Dean was not only a good manager but also a kind person, far different from the shadow of Jeff that had loomed in her mind. It was time to set aside her past feelings and embrace the present, focusing on building a positive working relationship with Dean.

By the end of the week, Maria felt a sense of accomplishment. Despite the challenges and her initial reservations, she had navigated through them with resilience. As she walked out of the supermarket, she felt a newfound confidence.

Chapter 8: Harmonies in the Night

The clubhouse within the compound was buzzing with excitement as Pete's birthday celebration reached its peak. The air was filled with laughter, clinking glasses, and the sounds of karaoke—a beloved activity among the Filipinos gathered there. Colorful streamers and balloons added a festive touch, and the aroma of delicious food wafted through the air.

Maria, Teresa, and Christine were gathered near the karaoke machine, chatting and enjoying the lively atmosphere. Pete, the birthday celebrant, was mingling with guests, his face glowing with happiness. Alfred, the store's manager, was seated nearby, sharing a drink with Edgar and Noel, their conversations punctuated with hearty laughter.

"Alright, Teresa, your turn!" Edgar called out, nudging Teresa toward the microphone. Teresa laughed and shook her head.

"No, no," she said, holding up her hands. "I'm no good at this. But Maria here, she's got a voice that'll knock your socks off!"

"Yeah, Maria, come on!" Christine encouraged, giving her a gentle push.

Maria felt a mix of nerves and excitement. Only Christine knew about her deep love for singing and her musical background. Taking a deep breath, she approached the karaoke machine.

"Alright, alright," Maria said, smiling at the cheers and clapping from her friends. "I'll give it a try."

"Show them what you've got!" Teresa cheered, giving her a thumbs-up.

With practiced ease, Maria selected her favorite song, *"Breakaway"* by Kelly Clarkson. As the familiar melody began, she felt a wave of calm wash over her. Singing had always been her sanctuary, a cherished part of her life since childhood. Her family was known for their musical talents, and she had been a key member of school choirs and often sang during school masses.

As Maria's voice filled the room, the crowd fell silent, entranced by her performance. Her voice was clear and powerful, each note imbued with emotion. She sang with a passion that captivated everyone, revealing her love for music and her incredible talent.

The room erupted in applause as she finished, and Maria blushed, giving a shy smile and a small bow.

"That was incredible, Maria!" Christine exclaimed, pulling her into a hug. "You were amazing!"

"Seriously," Teresa added, shaking her head in disbelief. "Why didn't you tell us you could sing like that?"

Maria shrugged modestly. "I just enjoy singing. It's something I've always loved to do, especially with my family."

"Well, you should do it more often," Pete said, raising his glass in a toast. "That was fantastic!"

Alfred, who had been listening from his seat, nodded in agreement. "You've got a real gift, Maria. That was truly something special."

Edgar clapped her on the back. "We need to have karaoke nights more often if it means hearing you sing!"

Noel, always the joker, added with a grin, "I think you just set the bar too high for the rest of us!"

The camaraderie and warmth in the room were palpable, and Maria felt a deep sense of belonging and joy. The celebration continued, with more songs and laughter filling the night.

As the evening wore on, Maria, Teresa, and Christine found a quieter corner to chat.

"That was so much fun," Teresa said, her eyes shining with happiness. "I haven't had such a great time in ages."

"Me neither," Christine agreed. "It's nights like these that make all the hard work worth it."

Maria nodded, her heart full. "I'm glad we're all here together. It's like having a little family away from home."

"Speaking of family," Teresa said, looking at Maria with a knowing smile. "What's going on with you and Dean? I saw the way he was looking at you while you were singing."

Maria blushed, shaking her head. "Nothing's going on. He's just being friendly."

"Uh-huh," Christine said, giving her a playful nudge. "Well, if he asks you out for a drink, you should go. He seems like a nice guy."

Before Maria could respond, her phone buzzed in her pocket. She pulled it out and read the message from Dean: "Hi Maria, I didn't know you have such an amazing voice! You still up for a drink or two?"

Teresa, glancing over Maria's shoulder, caught sight of the message and raised an eyebrow. "Speak of the devil," she teased. "Looks like he's already making his move."

Christine chuckled, giving Maria an encouraging smile. "Go on, Maria. Have a drink with him. We'll catch up with you later."

Maria hesitated for a moment, then replied to Dean: "Sure, let's have a drink."

Dean's response was quick: "Meet me at the bar in the clubhouse?"

Maria looked across the room and saw Dean waiting by the bar, a warm smile on his face. She nodded, feeling a mix of curiosity and anticipation.

"Good luck," Teresa whispered, giving her a wink as Maria stood up.

Maria walked over to Dean, who handed her a glass as she approached. "To an unforgettable performance," he toasted, clinking his glass with hers.

"Thanks, Dean," Maria said, feeling a bit shy under his admiring gaze. "I didn't know you enjoyed karaoke."

"I do, especially when there's real talent like yours on display," Dean replied warmly. "How long have you been singing?"

"For as long as I can remember," Maria replied, taking a sip of her drink. "My family is really into music. We've always been singing together, and I was part of the school choir for years."

"That's amazing," Dean said, his eyes lighting up with interest. "I used to play guitar in a band during college, but we were never as good as you."

"You were in a band?" Maria asked, surprised. "What kind of music did you play?"

"A bit of everything," Dean said with a nostalgic smile. "Rock, pop, whatever we felt like. It was a lot of fun, but nothing serious."

Maria laughed softly. "It sounds like you had a great time."

Dean nodded. "I did. Music has a way of bringing people together, doesn't it?"

"It really does," Maria agreed, feeling more relaxed. "I love how it connects us and creates such wonderful memories."

As they continued to share stories, Maria and Dean discovered they had much in common—their love for music, their appreciation for simple joys, and even some shared experiences in managing retail operations. Maria found herself enjoying Dean's company, their conversation flowing easily.

Dean looked at her thoughtfully. "You know, Maria, I've been meaning to talk to you about something."

Maria raised an eyebrow, curious. "What is it?"

"I was wondering if you'd like to go out to dinner with me sometime," Dean said, his smile hopeful. "There's a nice restaurant nearby, quite safe for expats like us, tight security and all. I'd really like to get to know you better."

Maria felt a flutter of excitement in her chest. However, in the back of her mind, Maria couldn't shake off a hint of reluctance. It had only been five months since her breakup with Jeff, and she wasn't sure if she had fully moved on. But as she looked into Dean's eyes, she realized that it was worth giving a chance. "I'd really like that," she repeated, her heart feeling a little lighter. "Let's do dinner sometime." With that, Maria smiled, feeling a sense of excitement for the possibilities ahead.

Chapter 9: A Secret Affair

Maria couldn't believe that it had already been three months since she and Dean had started their secret relationship. Dean was the kind of person who preferred to keep his personal life private, so they hadn't told anyone about their romance, not even her close friend Christine. Whenever Christine prodded, Maria would brush off their closeness as merely a strong friendship, citing mundane excuses like discussing stocktake discrepancies. It was a flimsy cover, but Maria stuck to it.

Even Maria's family remained in the dark about her budding relationship; it was still too early to share such news. Going out for dinner together had to be kept clandestine. Luckily, Dean's position as a senior manager afforded them the freedom to slip away unnoticed, thanks to his access to the gate and knowledge of security protocols.

Their moments together were often stolen in the office during Teresa's busy hours, ensuring that their staff didn't interfere with their bosses' business. Alternatively, they'd find solace in the warehouse liquor room, where Dean would occasionally call Maria on the radio or send a discreet text, just to steal a kiss.

In most cases, Maria would arrive at the office early to ensure they had more time together before the day began. Despite the secrecy, Maria and Dean had mastered the art of maintaining their relationship, even creating a secret Facebook account where they could share their photos together without raising suspicions. Dean had also been remarkably supportive of Maria's efforts to assist her family. Once, when Maria mentioned her desire for a separate bedroom in their house, Dean didn't hesitate to offer financial assistance. He even contributed money during her parents' birthdays, which happened to fall on consecutive dates. Initially, Maria was hesitant to accept his help, but Dean insisted, showing his generosity without reservation.

Maria couldn't help but notice that Dean's way of expressing love seemed to be through gift-giving. Despite her initial reluctance, she began to understand and appreciate his gestures, realizing that his actions spoke volumes about his affection for her and her family.

As the days passed, Maria found herself falling deeper in love with Dean, cherishing every stolen moment they shared.

Chapter 10: Shadows in Celebration

Preparations for Papua New Guinea's Independence Day were in full swing, with Alfred leading a meeting to discuss decorating the stores with the national theme, traditional costumes for the staff, and a special staff presentation.

Alfred emphasized the importance of capturing the spirit of PNG's Independence Day in the stores.

"Alright everyone, let's make sure we showcase our culture and celebrate our nation's pride. Maria, I need you to coordinate with the staff and ensure everything is ready."

Meanwhile, Rey returned to the supermarket as a reliever while Dean went back to the Philippines to visit his sick father. Alfred kept an eye on Rey's store, knowing it was smaller than Maria's.

"It's good to be back, Maria. How's everything going?" Rey asked.

"Busy as always. We're gearing up for Independence Day," Maria replied.

Maria missed Dean a lot but understood why he hadn't been in touch much; he was busy caring for his father. Their last conversation was two days ago when he went out to meet friends.

As the day of celebration approached, the preparations intensified. Maria enlisted the help of some staff, engaging them in decorating the stores with enthusiasm.

In the evening, Christine, Teresa, and Maria discussed the final touches for the celebrations and the staff presentation.

The Independence Day festivities began with a vibrant parade around the stores. Staff adorned in traditional costumes marched proudly, with managers following in a car. The atmosphere was filled with excitement and joy as Pete distributed cash prizes, and Alfred and Noel organized games.

As the day came to a close, Maria, Christine, and Teresa shared a moment of reflection.

"Today was amazing, wasn't it? I'm proud of our team," Maria remarked.

"Definitely. Everyone put in so much effort," Christine agreed.

"It's moments like these that bring us together," Teresa added.

Later, as Maria was about to sleep, her phone beeped with a message from Dean. Excitedly, she opened it, only to be met with shock and hurt as she saw a screenshot of their Facebook page with a derogatory message at the bottom: *"Slut!"*

Chapter 11: Betrayed

Maria felt like she had been doused with icy water. Everything came crashing down around her. How could she have been so blind, so utterly stupid? The harsh reality of Dean's betrayal hit her with the force of a storm. Dean was married. He had a wife and a son. How could she have not known?

In her naivety, Maria had believed that Dean's insistence on keeping their relationship private was out of a desire to protect their budding romance. Now, she understood the bitter truth: he was hiding his infidelity. She replayed their conversations in her mind, searching for any signs she had missed. It was her fault, she thought, for allowing herself to be swept away by her emotions without truly knowing who Dean was.

Messages from Dean's wife flooded her phone, each one more venomous than the last. Maria's attempts to explain, to assure her that she hadn't known about Dean's double life, fell on deaf ears. The wife's fury was relentless, her mind closed to any form of explanation.

Dean's wife wrote to Maria with fiery words, calling her names and accusing her of ruining their family. "You knew he was married, how could you do this?" she typed furiously. Maria's fingers trembled as she replied, trying to keep her voice steady. "I didn't know. I swear I didn't know. If I had known, I would never have let this happen." But it was no use. Dean's wife was beyond reason.

The situation worsened dramatically when Dean's wife sent all their private messages and photos to Pete and Alfred via email. Maria's heart sank as she realized the extent of the exposure. The entire supermarket staff would know about the scandal by morning. Dean wasn't even there to face the consequences with her. She was left to bear the brunt of the fallout alone.

Maria couldn't sleep. Thoughts of how to face her colleagues and her family churned in her mind. What would she tell them? How could she explain? Her career, her dreams—everything she had worked so hard for—seemed to be crumbling.

The next day at work was torture. Maria felt a deep sense of isolation and discomfort. Although Teresa and Christine, who used to be her closest confidantes, often exchanged glances and whispered among themselves, their expressions were filled with concern rather than malice. Maria misinterpreted their somber looks and hushed conversations as judgmental stares, unaware that they were actually worried about her well-being. Instead of the usual light-hearted banter, their subdued demeanor reflected a genuine sense of sorrow for her. The silence that enveloped her as they passed her desk was not one of condemnation, but rather of empathetic sorrow, making Maria feel more isolated than ever.

They knew. Everyone knew. And now, the office, which once felt like a safe haven, had turned cold and unwelcoming. Maria couldn't escape the feeling that she had become an outsider, judged and isolated by those she once considered friends.

In the middle of the day, Rey, who had recently returned to cover Dean's duties, approached Maria. His usually warm demeanor was replaced with a mix of concern and bewilderment. "Maria, what's going on? I heard something, but I can't believe it. Is it true?"

Maria tried to hold back tears. "It's true, Rey. Dean... he lied to me. He's married. I didn't know."

Rey looked at her, a deep sadness in his eyes. "I don't know what to say. We all thought you were just... colleagues. Maybe close friends. But this..."

Maria nodded, feeling the weight of his disappointment. "I didn't know, Rey. I thought I knew him."

Later, Teresa found a quiet moment to approach Maria. "Maria, why didn't you tell us? We were just joking about Dean. If we had known it was serious, we could have helped you understand what was really going on."

Maria could only whisper, "I thought I was in love. I thought he was, too." She felt tears sting her eyes, but she blinked them away, unwilling to break down in front of Teresa.

Christine wasn't far behind. She pulled Maria aside, her voice a mix of shock and sadness. "You were always so careful. How could you let this happen? Why didn't you tell me? Maybe I could have helped you see..."

Maria's voice trembled as she replied, "I thought we had something real. I didn't want to ruin it with gossip."

Maria looked at Teresa and Christine, feeling a mix of frustration and disbelief. She couldn't shake the feeling that they were trying to justify their previous teasing about Dean, a married man. However, caught in the throes of her own pain, Maria might have been misinterpreting their intentions. Their attempts to explain themselves and downplay the seriousness of the situation could have been genuine efforts to mend their friendship, but Maria's sense of betrayal and hurt clouded her judgment. In her current state, it was difficult for her to see past her own suffering to understand their possible remorse and concern.

As the day dragged on, Maria couldn't shake the feeling that everyone around her was whispering about her. The constant hum of conversations seemed to fill the air with unspoken judgments. However, the truth was far less dramatic; her colleagues were absorbed in their own work and conversations that had nothing to do with her. Yet, Maria's distress made her imagine gossip swirling around her like daggers in her back. Her perception of her reputation and dignity being in tatters was a reflection of her inner turmoil, not the reality of her workplace.

Rey tried to offer a small measure of comfort, "Look, Maria, I don't know what's going to happen, but you need to stay strong. We'll figure this out."

But Maria could only nod, knowing that her future was now uncertain. Her reputation, her dignity—all were in tatters.

That night, Maria sank onto her bed, the phone slipping from her grasp. The betrayal cut deeper than any wound. How could Dean, the man she thought she loved, do this to her? How could he allow his wife to attack her like this? She had so many questions, so many thoughts racing through her mind.

As she lay there, staring at the ceiling, she felt the crushing weight of her shattered dreams pressing down on her chest. The prospect of facing her colleagues again filled her with dread, even though their whispered conversations likely had nothing to do with her. The thought of explaining everything to her family added to her anxiety. In her state of anguish, she couldn't see that her fears of isolation and judgment were amplified by her inner turmoil. Though she felt profoundly alone and as if the life she had carefully built was crumbling, it was possible that this perception was more a reflection of her emotional pain than the reality around her.

Chapter 12: A Heartfelt Confession

Maria sat on the edge of her bed, her phone trembling in her hands as she prepared to make the call she had been dreading. The familiar faces of her parents appeared on the screen, their expressions warm and welcoming. She couldn't hold back the tears any longer. She took a deep breath and tried to steady her voice.

"Mama, Papa, I need to tell you something," Maria began, her voice shaking with emotion.

Her mother's face immediately filled with concern. "Maria, what's wrong? Why are you crying?" she asked, leaning closer to the screen.

Her father looked equally worried. "Yes, *anak*, what's going on?"

Maria wiped her tears with the back of her hand, trying to find the right words. "It's about Dean," she said softly, her voice cracking. "I... I was in a relationship with him. I thought we had something special. But I didn't know he was married."

Her parents exchanged shocked glances, their faces reflecting a mix of confusion and disbelief.

Her mother was the first to speak. "Married? Oh, Maria, how could this happen? How did you not know?"

Maria felt a fresh wave of tears. "He kept our relationship private. He said he wanted to keep things quiet because he's a reserved person. I believed him. But then his wife found out about us and... she's been sending me horrible messages."

Her father's brow furrowed in concern. "What kind of messages?" he asked gently.

"She called me... awful names," Maria whispered, her voice barely audible. "She even sent evidence of our relationship to my bosses. Now everyone at work knows."

Her mother's face softened, and she reached out as if to touch Maria through the screen. "Oh, my sweet girl, we had no idea you were going through this. You didn't do anything wrong by believing in him. You trusted him."

Maria felt a sob escape her lips. "I feel so stupid. I should have known. How could I have been so blind?"

Her father spoke up, his voice firm but loving. "Maria, you were deceived. This is not your fault. You followed your heart, and he took advantage of that."

Her mother nodded in agreement. "We love you, Maria, and we're here for you. You haven't failed us. We're proud of you for being brave enough to tell us the truth."

Maria's heart ached at their words. She had feared their disappointment more than anything, but their unwavering support gave her a glimmer of hope. "Thank you," she whispered, her voice filled with gratitude. "I don't know what to do next. Dean has gone back to the Philippines, and I'm left here alone to face all of this."

Her father leaned closer, his eyes filled with determination. "We'll figure this out together. You're not alone. Whatever you decide, we'll support you."

Her mother added softly, "Take it one step at a time. We're with you every step of the way."

As she sat alone in her room later that night, the weight of her decisions pressed down on her. With her reputation tarnished and the judgment of her colleagues weighing heavily on her, Maria knew she couldn't stay at the supermarket any longer. Resigning seemed like the only option.

But where would she go? She couldn't bear the thought of returning to the Philippines, not with the life she had built here, not with the dreams she had begun to chase.

Maria turned to her faith for solace. She knelt by her bed and clasped her hands, praying to God for guidance. "Please, Lord, help me find the strength to get through this," she whispered, her voice trembling with emotion.

She then prayed to the Blessed Mother, seeking her gentle comfort. "Mary, please watch over me and give me the grace to endure this pain," she murmured, tears slipping down her cheeks.

Finally, she prayed to St. Michael, the defender. "St. Michael, protect me from harm and give me the courage to face this battle," she pleaded, feeling a sense of peace wash over her.

The next day, Maria was startled when Rey approached her with news. "Maria, I heard something," he said quietly, his voice filled with apprehension. "Dean has resigned. He's not coming back."

Maria's heart skipped a beat at the revelation. Despite everything, she couldn't help but feel a pang of longing for Dean. She wanted closure, she wanted answers, but with Dean gone and his wife out of reach, she knew it was impossible.

With a heavy sigh, Maria made her decision. She would endure the cold stares and harsh judgments of her colleagues until she found a way out. She would bear the weight of her mistakes alone, determined to find a new path forward, no matter how uncertain it may be.

Chapter 13: A Glimmer of Hope

Maria tried to keep her composure and act as though everything was fine, despite the turmoil in her personal life. To distract herself from the silent judgments and whispers around her, she threw herself into the day-to-day retail operations at the supermarket. She often left her office to help on the store floor, hoping that staying busy would keep her mind off her troubles. Over time, she got accustomed to the rhythm of the daily tasks and the constant buzz of activity in the store.

One afternoon, while she was meticulously checking the gondola ends and making sure they were well-stocked, Ross approached her. Ross was a Malaysian manager from Lae who had been in Popondetta for a week to monitor his company's product sales.

Initially, Ross was all about the numbers and the performance of his products. But as the days passed, he couldn't help but notice Maria's dedication and precision in her work. Every day, he observed how she managed the displays with such care and efficiency. Gradually, his interest shifted from just monitoring sales to genuinely appreciating Maria's work ethic and commitment.

"Hi Maria," Ross greeted warmly as he approached the display. "I've noticed you've been doing a fantastic job with our tuna products. The gondola end always looks so well-organized and inviting."

Maria looked up and gave a small smile. "Thanks, Ross. I just want to make sure everything is set up properly and that it helps boost sales."

Ross nodded, clearly impressed. "That's actually why I wanted to ask if we could purchase more space on the gondola end for our tuna products. The way you've arranged them has really been helping."

Maria thought for a moment. "I'll check on the availability and see if we can allocate more space for your products. I think we can work something out."

Over the next few days, Ross made a point to have more conversations with Maria. Initially, his visits were all about business, but as they talked more, their exchanges became friendlier and more personal. Maria noticed his frequent appearances but attributed them to his thoroughness in ensuring his products performed well.

One day, during one of their routine check-ins, Ross brought up something that caught Maria's attention. "I was in Port Moresby recently," he said, "interviewing candidates for a sales and marketing executive position in Lae. Unfortunately, none of them were a good fit."

Maria's curiosity was piqued. "Is the position still open?" she asked, sensing an opportunity. "I've been thinking about exploring new roles, and that sounds interesting."

Ross looked at her thoughtfully. Over the past week, he had been increasingly impressed by her. "Yes, it's still open," he replied. "Given how well you handle sales and your marketing acumen, I think you'd be a strong candidate. I could arrange a virtual interview with our team if you're interested."

Maria felt a spark of hope. "That sounds perfect," she said, her excitement barely contained. "I would love to apply. Thank you, Ross."

Ross smiled. "You've shown great skill and dedication, Maria. I'm sure you'd excel in the role. I'll talk to my boss and see about setting up the interview."

Over the following days, Ross continued to visit the store, not just to keep tabs on the product displays but also to support Maria in the application process. His admiration for her work and his willingness to help gave Maria a much-needed boost of confidence.

Later in the week, as they were discussing the details of the gondola end, Ross brought up the interview again. "I spoke with my boss," he said. "He's really interested in your application and suggested we do a virtual interview. We can schedule it for next week if that works for you."

"That sounds great," Maria responded, her spirits lifting. "Thank you so much, Ross. I really appreciate your help."

"It's the least I can do," Ross replied with a smile. "You've demonstrated impressive knowledge in sales and marketing. I'm confident you'll do well."

With the prospect of a new job on the horizon, Maria felt a renewed sense of purpose. She poured herself into her work with even more determination, finding solace in the busy hours and the hope of a fresh start in Lae.

Chapter 14: New Beginnings in Lae

Maria stood at the window of her new room, gazing out at the bustling cityscape of Lae. Unlike the quieter town of Popondetta, Lae was alive with the constant hum of city life. It was a new chapter in her journey, and she felt a mix of excitement and apprehension as she settled into her new role as sales and marketing executive at Oceanic International Ltd., a leading company in the tuna industry.

Lae was different in many ways, not just because it was a city but also because of the heightened security concerns for expatriates. Despite the company's efforts to ensure safety, Maria felt a twinge of anxiety, especially when she was out checking stock at various supermarkets without any security escort. One of the Malaysian managers would drop her off and pick her up when she was done, which often left her feeling vulnerable.

The company provided a house for its expatriate staff, and Maria quickly made herself at home. She shared the house with four colleagues: Heidi, Jean, Alex, and John. They were all from Mindanao, except for Heidi, who, like Maria, was from Luzon. The supervisors at Oceanic International Ltd. were Filipinos, while the higher management were all Malaysians, creating a unique blend of cultures within the company.

Maria quickly formed a close bond with Heidi, her roommate and colleague in the sales department. Heidi's easygoing nature and shared cultural background made her a comforting presence amid all the new faces and responsibilities.

Heidi smiled as she watched Maria unpacking. "How are you finding Lae so far?" she asked, sitting cross-legged on her bed.

"It's definitely different from Popondetta," Maria replied, hanging up her clothes. "More vibrant, but also more challenging in some ways. I miss the quiet sometimes."

Heidi nodded. "Lae can be overwhelming at first, but you'll get used to it. And don't worry about work; you'll do great. We'll figure things out together."

The work environment was another adjustment. Maria spent her days juggling her new responsibilities, often venturing out to various supermarkets to check on stock. This part of her job seemed unorthodox, as she wasn't always sure if it truly fell under her job description, but she approached it with determination.

During one of her stock visits, she called Heidi for advice. "Heidi, I'm at the store, and I'm not sure how to handle this inventory issue. Can you help?"

Heidi chuckled on the other end of the line. "Of course, Maria. Just take it one step at a time. Look at the sales reports first, and then we can figure out the next steps together."

The workdays were long and often daunting, especially since Ross had provided no formal training or orientation for her new role. Maria relied heavily on Heidi's guidance, learning the ropes through observation and persistence.

Despite the challenges at work, Maria enjoyed the cultural exchange that came with her new environment. She found herself fascinated by the mix of Malaysian and Mindanaoan cultures she encountered daily.

One particular incident stuck out in her mind. One evening, their CEO, Ahmad, discovered a package of frozen pork in the staff's communal freezer. Ahmad, who adhered strictly to his Muslim faith, was visibly upset and didn't speak to the Filipino staff for days.

Maria recalled how Heidi had explained the situation to her. " It's a big deal for him to find pork here," she said.

The pork was intended as a gift to a staff member. Later, they discovered that Ross had placed it there. Once the misunderstanding was cleared up, Ahmad resumed his usual interactions. However, the incident left a lasting impression on Maria, highlighting the importance of cultural sensitivity.

Maria also embraced new culinary experiences. She learned to enjoy *kinilaw*, a popular Filipino dish made of raw fish marinated in vinegar, calamansi juice, and spices. The freshness and zest of the dish quickly became one of her favorites.

Outside of work, Maria found solace in the strong Filipino community in Lae. Every Saturday and Sunday, they gathered at a local gym to play basketball and badminton. These gatherings were a highlight for Maria, offering a sense of belonging and a break from the pressures of her new job. The staff would carpool to the gym, utilizing a vehicle provided by the company for the Filipino expatriates.

During one such gathering, Maria met other Filipinos from different companies. They shared stories of their lives in Lae and offered tips on adjusting to the new environment.

John, one of her housemates, approached her during a break. "How's the new job treating you, Maria?" he asked, handing her a bottle of water.

"It's been challenging," she admitted. "But I'm learning a lot. And having a supportive community here makes it easier."

John nodded. "We've all been there. Just take it one day at a time. You're doing great."

Each weekend, Maria looked forward to these moments of camaraderie. They were a welcome respite from the hectic pace of work and the lingering shadows of her past.

One evening, after a particularly exhausting day, Maria settled into her room to call her family. Seeing their faces on the screen brought a wave of comfort.

"Mama, Papa," she began, her voice tinged with fatigue but also with a hint of pride. "I'm settling in here in Lae. The job is tough, but I'm managing."

Her mother's voice was filled with concern. "Are you okay, *anak*? You seem tired."

Maria smiled. "I'm okay, Mama. Just a lot to learn and adjust to. But I'm getting there. And I've made some good friends who are helping me along the way."

Her father's voice chimed in, reassuringly. "We're proud of you, Maria. Remember, we're always here for you."

After the call, as the city of Lae quieted down for the night, Maria knelt beside her bed and prayed. With each prayer, Maria felt a bit more grounded, a bit more prepared to face the challenges ahead. She knew that despite the obstacles, she was forging a path toward a brighter future, one step at a time.

In these moments of reflection, Maria realized that her family was her true source of strength. Their unwavering support and love were the anchors that kept her steady amid the storm. No matter how far she ventured from home, their faith in her was a constant reminder that she could overcome anything.

Chapter 15: A Trip to Remember

Excitement buzzed in the air as Maria and Heidi prepared for their upcoming five-day seminar in Kuala Lumpur, Malaysia. It would be their first time traveling to the country, and the anticipation was palpable.

"I can't believe we're actually going to Malaysia!" Heidi exclaimed, her eyes sparkling with excitement. "I've always wanted to see Kuala Lumpur."

Maria smiled, sharing in Heidi's enthusiasm. "Same here! I've heard so much about the city. It's going to be an amazing experience."

As they discussed their plans, Ross entered the room, interrupting their conversation with a professional demeanor.

"Ladies, I wanted to go over a few things regarding the seminar," Ross began. "The seminar is called 'Advanced Strategies in Sales and Marketing' and will be held at the Shangri-La Hotel in Kuala Lumpur. It's a five-star venue, so expect top-notch accommodations."

He continued, outlining their itinerary and what they should prepare. "Our flight leaves early tomorrow morning. Make sure you have all your travel documents ready. We'll be covering a range of topics, from market analysis to digital sales techniques. It's a fantastic opportunity for both of you."

Heidi nodded eagerly. "We're ready, Ross. Thank you for arranging everything."

Ross smiled, a rare show of warmth. "It's part of my job to ensure you get the best training. And besides, this is a great chance for us to bond as a team."

The next morning, Maria and Heidi were up before dawn, brimming with excitement as they boarded their flight to Malaysia. The journey was smooth, and they marveled at the sight of Kuala Lumpur's skyline as they descended into the bustling metropolis.

Kuala Lumpur was a city of contrasts, where modern skyscrapers stood alongside historic temples and colonial-era architecture. The streets were vibrant, teeming with people from diverse backgrounds. It was a melting pot of cultures, with the cosmopolitan vibe that resonated through every corner.

As they arrived at the opulent Shangri-La Hotel, Maria couldn't help but be impressed. The marble floors gleamed under the chandeliers, and the staff greeted them with warm smiles. Their rooms were luxurious, with views overlooking the city.

"This place is incredible," Heidi said, her eyes wide as she took in their surroundings. "I feel like we're in a movie."

Maria laughed. "It's definitely a step up from our usual digs in Lae."

The seminar kicked off the next day, bringing together professionals from around the world. The sessions were intense, packed with insights and strategies that left Maria and Heidi both exhausted and inspired.

During their first evening in Kuala Lumpur, Ross took them to try local cuisine at a bustling food market. Maria savored the flavors of *nasi lemak*, a fragrant rice dish cooked in coconut milk and served with spicy sambal, anchovies, peanuts, boiled egg, and cucumber. It was a new taste sensation that she quickly grew to love.

"This is amazing," Maria said, taking another bite. "I've never tasted anything like it."

Ross nodded in agreement. "Malaysian food is incredibly diverse. You can find influences from Chinese, Indian, and Malay cuisines all in one dish."

On their second evening, Ross played tour guide, taking them to some of Kuala Lumpur's famous attractions. They marveled at the Petronas Twin Towers, the world's tallest twin skyscrapers, and wandered through the bustling streets of Bukit Bintang, Kuala Lumpur's vibrant shopping and entertainment district. They also visited the Batu Caves, a series of limestone caves and temples guarded by a towering golden statue of Lord Murugan.

"Look at the view from up here," Ross said, standing with Maria and Heidi at the top of the Batu Caves steps. "Kuala Lumpur is a beautiful city."

Heidi snapped photos enthusiastically. "It's stunning. Thank you for showing us around, Ross."

Ross smiled. "It's my pleasure. I wanted you to experience the best of Malaysia while we're here."

As the seminar progressed, Maria and Heidi found themselves immersed in learning. Day four was particularly intense, with each team presenting their projects. Maria's team excelled, their presentation earning high praise from the seminar leaders.

Ross was visibly impressed. "You two did an outstanding job," he said after their presentation. "I'm proud of your hard work."

To celebrate, Ross took them out for drinks that evening. The atmosphere was lively, and spirits were high as they toasted their success. Heidi, however, had a bit too much to drink and ended up getting quite tipsy.

"Maybe we should head back," Maria suggested gently, noticing Heidi's increasingly unsteady demeanor.

Ross agreed, and they helped Heidi into a car. As they made their way back to the hotel, Heidi passed out, leaving Maria and Ross to manage her.

Back at the hotel, Ross and Maria struggled to get Heidi up to their room. Once they finally laid her down on the bed, Ross turned to Maria with an unexpected seriousness.

"Maria, there's something I've been wanting to ask you," he began, reaching into his pocket.

Maria looked at him, puzzled. "What is it, Ross?"

To her shock, Ross pulled out a small velvet box and opened it, revealing a sparkling ring. "Will you marry me?"

Maria's heart pounded with uncertainty as she contemplated Ross's proposal. The weight of his words hung heavy in the air, stirring a whirlwind of emotions within her. Was this the culmination of his intentions all along? Or was there more to his sudden proposal than met the eye? She couldn't shake off the feeling of unease, grappling with the realization that Ross, a man with three wives, had extended his hand in marriage to her. It was a proposition she never imagined, one that veered sharply from the life she had envisioned for herself.

"Ross, I…I don't know what to say," Maria stammered, trying to process the situation. "I appreciate your feelings, but I can't. This isn't the life I dreamed of."

Ross's expression hardened. "But why not? I can take care of you. You'll have everything you want."

Maria shook her head, her voice trembling. "I'm sorry, Ross. I can't. I want something else for my life."

Ross's face darkened, but he said nothing more. He quietly left the room, leaving Maria in a whirlwind of emotions.

The next day, their flight back to Lae was filled with an uncomfortable silence. Ross's demeanor had shifted, and he treated Maria with a cold indifference. Maria felt the weight of his rejection but remained resolute. She knew she had made the right decision.

Upon their return to Lae, Maria exhaled deeply, prepared to confront whatever lay ahead. With a newfound determination, she resolved to chart her own course, remaining true to herself even in the face of potential obstacles and uncertainties.

Chapter 16: Home Away from Home

It was a typical Saturday afternoon at the gym in Lae. Maria and Heidi, accompanied by their friend Denise, were winding down after a rigorous badminton game.

"That was a tough match," Denise said, wiping sweat from her forehead. "You guys really pushed me to my limits today!"

Heidi laughed, "You were amazing out there, Denise. I thought I had you with that last smash."

Maria nodded in agreement, "Denise, your reflexes are incredible. I need to work on my net play to keep up with you."

As they chatted, two tall guys walked over to them. One of them had a basketball tucked under his arm.

"Hey, Denise," the guy with the basketball greeted her with a warm smile. "Great game. I could hear you guys from across the court."

"Thanks, Arnold," Denise beamed. "Maria, Heidi, this is Arnold, my boyfriend. And this is Franz, his teammate and a good friend of ours."

Maria and Heidi shook hands with Arnold and Franz. Maria's face lit up when she learned that Franz was also from Pampanga, her home province in the Philippines.

"So, you're a Kapampangan too?" Maria asked, her eyes sparkling with interest.

"Yep," Franz replied with a grin. "It's great to meet a fellow Kapampangan here in Lae. There are quite a few of us around. We usually gather every weekend at Arvin's place—he's a Kapampangan as well. We eat, drink, and, of course, sing karaoke."

Heidi chuckled, "Karaoke, huh? Sounds like a lot of fun."

Franz nodded enthusiastically. "You should join us sometime. In fact, we're heading over there later today. Friends of friends are always welcome. Just bring a pizza or two, and you're in. If you don't have a driver, I can pick you up and drop you off after the gathering."

Maria and Heidi exchanged glances. The idea of meeting more Kapampangans and enjoying a casual gathering was tempting.

"Why not?" Maria shrugged, smiling. "We could use a break from our usual routine."

"Great!" Franz exclaimed. "Arvin's place is not far from here. You'll love it. And by the way, we call ourselves the Pampanga Dragons. Even our basketball team goes by that name."

Later that evening, Maria, Heidi, and Denise found themselves at Arvin's house, a cozy place buzzing with the laughter and chatter of fellow Kapampangans. Franz introduced them to everyone: Jun and his girlfriend April, Nestor, Elmer and his wife Lorna, Berna, and Arvin, the gracious host.

"It's wonderful to meet all of you," Maria said warmly as she shook hands and exchanged hugs. "I never expected to find such a tight-knit community of Kapampangans here in Lae."

Arvin, a stocky man with a friendly demeanor, nodded. "We're a small group, but we stick together. It's our way of keeping a piece of home alive while we're here."

The evening progressed with the comforting sounds of laughter and the familiar melodies of Filipino karaoke. As they sang and enjoyed the spread of food—*crispy pata, adobo,* and other Filipino delicacies—Maria felt a sense of belonging she hadn't experienced since leaving Popondetta.

During a break from the singing, the conversation turned to the upcoming election of the Filipino Association in Lae.

"We're preparing for the elections next month," Franz mentioned as he refilled his drink. "I'm planning to run for president, and Arnold here is going to be my vice president."

Denise nodded, adding, "We've been trying to find someone to run as secretary. I would have loved to do it, but my job as a general manager keeps me too busy."

Maria listened intently, feeling a growing curiosity about the association's activities.

"Have you found anyone yet?" she asked.

Franz shook his head. "Not yet. We've been asking around, but most people are too busy or not interested."

Denise suddenly turned to Maria with a thoughtful look. "What about you, Maria? You could run for secretary."

Maria was taken aback. "Me? But I'm new here, and I don't know many people."

Arnold smiled reassuringly. "That could actually work in your favor. Sometimes, a fresh face brings new perspectives. And from what I've heard, you have a background in teaching, which means you're organized and good with people."

Heidi nodded in agreement. "Plus, you have the support of all of us. We can help you with the campaign."

Maria hesitated, considering their words. "I'll think about it. It's a big responsibility, and I want to make sure I'm ready for it."

The night continued with more singing and stories. Maria felt a deep connection with her newfound friends. For the first time in a while, the stress from work and her recent troubles faded into the background. Here, among fellow Filipinos, she found a sense of home and community that gave her strength.

Later, as the night came to an end, Maria walked back to her apartment with Heidi. The evening's joy and camaraderie left her feeling light-hearted and hopeful. She might have left her old life behind, but she was building something new and meaningful here in Lae.

Chapter 17: Navigating New Waters

Franz stood at the front of the room, his voice clear and authoritative, as he brought the meeting to a close. "Alright, everyone, that's it for today. Thank you for your support. Let's make this term a great one for our community. Meeting adjourned!"

Maria sat beside him, the newly elected secretary of the Filipino Association in Lae. As the members began to gather their belongings, she reflected on how quickly things had changed. It felt surreal to think about the journey that had led her to this point, especially how she had hesitated to join the association in the first place.

She exchanged a quick glance with Franz, who had navigated his first meeting as president with ease. The room was filled with the familiar faces of the Pampanga Dragons, a community that had embraced her and made Lae feel like home. It was all thanks to Franz's encouragement that she had taken on this role.

Later, as the room emptied out, Maria and Franz stayed behind to wrap up the final details. Franz smiled at Maria, a hint of admiration in his eyes. "You did great today, Secretary Maria. Handling all those minutes and organizing everyone like that—it's impressive."

Maria blushed slightly, looking down at her notes. "Thanks, Franz. I still can't believe how fast everything's happened. It feels like just yesterday we were talking about the elections, and now here we are."

Franz chuckled. "Time flies when you're making a difference. Speaking of which, how are you settling in at work? I know things have been a bit... chilly with Ross."

Maria sighed, thinking about Ross's continued coldness. "It's manageable. I keep it professional, and Heidi's been a big help. But I'm just trying to stay focused and not let it get to me."

Franz nodded, his expression thoughtful. "You've been handling it really well. And if you ever need to talk or need help with anything, I'm here. Just like the association, we're a team now."

Outside the office, Maria's life had become a whirlwind of activity. With her role in the association, she found herself busier than ever. The once regular four-times-a-week video calls with her family had dwindled to just twice a month. She missed them terribly but was often too caught up in her responsibilities to keep in touch as much as she would have liked.

She and Franz were growing closer, their bond deepening with each project they worked on together. He had a way of making her laugh and feel at ease, a welcome change from the tension she often felt at work. Their dinners had become a daily ritual, and Franz was always there to pick her up, ensuring she had company and a sense of security in her new environment.

One evening, as they wrapped up another dinner, Franz looked at Maria with a hint of something more in his eyes. "You know, Maria, I really enjoy our time together. You're someone special, and I'm glad to have met you."

Maria smiled, though a part of her wondered if there was more to his words. "I feel the same way, Franz. You've made Lae feel like home."

Their closeness hadn't gone unnoticed. At work, Ross had started to favor Heidi with more responsibilities and perks, seemingly in response to seeing Franz's attention towards Maria. It was a subtle shift, but Maria could sense the tension.

One day, as they were finishing up a meeting, Ross glanced over at Maria, his expression unreadable. "I see Franz has been keeping you busy outside of work too."

Maria stiffened slightly but kept her tone neutral. "Franz and I are friends. He's been helping me adjust to life here."

Ross nodded slowly. "Just make sure it doesn't interfere with your job. We have a lot of work ahead."

Maria forced a smile. "Of course, Ross. I'm committed to my work here."

That night, Maria finally made time to call her family. Seeing their faces on the screen brought a wave of relief and homesickness.

Her sister, Lucy, was the first to speak. "*Ate*, you look so busy! How's everything going?"

Maria laughed softly. "Busy is an understatement. But it's good. I'm learning a lot and meeting so many new people."

Her brother, Miguel, chimed in. "And what about Franz? You mentioned him before. Is he just a friend?"

Maria hesitated, thinking about their growing closeness. "He's a good friend. He's been really supportive, especially with all the changes."

Her parents exchanged a knowing look. "Just be careful, *anak*," her mother said gently. "You've been through a lot already."

Maria nodded, feeling a lump in her throat. "I know, Mama. I'm just taking it one day at a time."

As the call ended, Maria felt a renewed sense of strength. Her family's support and love were her anchors, giving her the courage to navigate the challenges ahead.

As they hung up, she whispered a silent prayer, grateful for the connections she had both back home and in her new life in Lae. No matter the challenges, she knew she had the strength to face them, surrounded by a community that felt like a home away from home.

Chapter 18: Breaking Point

The sky was a canvas of deep purples and pinks as the sun set over Lae. Maria and Franz sat quietly on a bench near the waterfront, the tranquility of the scene offering a brief respite from the day's events. The gentle hum of the city winding down provided a soothing backdrop as they took in the view.

Franz turned to Maria, his expression serious yet soft. "Maria, there's something I've been wanting to tell you," he began, his voice carrying a weight of emotion. "I really like you, more than just a friend. I've felt this way for a while now."

Maria's heart skipped a beat. She had sensed Franz's growing affection, but hearing it spoken aloud made it all the more real. She looked at him, searching for the right words. "Franz, I like you too," she confessed softly. "But I've been through so much lately. I'm not sure if I'm ready for a relationship."

Franz's eyes were full of understanding. "I get it, Maria. You've had a lot on your plate. I'm not asking you to make a decision right now. I just wanted to be honest with you about my feelings. I'm willing to wait, no matter how long it takes."

Maria felt a warm rush of gratitude. "Thank you, Franz. That means a lot. I'll think about it, I promise."

As they stood up to leave, Maria felt a mix of uncertainty and hope. Lae had brought many unexpected twists into her life, and this was yet another she would have to navigate carefully.

The following morning, the usual hum of activity at work was replaced by an uneasy quiet. News had spread quickly that a Filipino expatriate had been shot by a local rascal at the town market earlier in the day. Thankfully, the suspect had been arrested and the expat had been rushed to the hospital and was reported to be stable.

"Did you hear about the shooting?" Heidi asked as she joined Maria in the break room, her face reflecting the shared anxiety of their community.

"Yes, it's awful," Maria replied, her voice tinged with worry. "I hope he recovers quickly."

Heidi nodded, looking around as if seeking reassurance. "It's terrifying. We have to be so careful now. I can't believe it happened so close to us."

The news cast a shadow over the day, making everyone acutely aware of the fragile sense of security they had in Lae.

Later that afternoon, Maria's phone buzzed with a message from Ross. She felt a knot tighten in her stomach as she read his instructions. He wanted her to go to town and check the stock levels at a warehouse, despite the day's unsettling events.

"Ross, can I have a security escort?" Maria asked when she entered his office, her voice steady but tinged with apprehension. "Given what happened this morning, I don't feel safe going alone."

Ross leaned back in his chair, a faint smirk playing on his lips. "No security," he replied dismissively. "If something happens, well, that's just the risk you have to take."

Maria's heart sank at his callousness. She felt a surge of anger but knew better than to argue. She took a deep breath and left his office, determined to complete the task quickly.

At the warehouse, her anxiety made it hard to focus. She hurried through the inventory, her mind racing with thoughts of the shooting and Ross's indifference to her safety. In her rush, she miscounted the stock levels.

When she returned to report, Ross's expression turned icy. "You miscounted the stocks, Maria. This is unacceptable. Are you incapable of doing anything right?"

The insult cut deep. Maria's face flushed with anger. "I did my best, Ross. Given the circumstances, it was hard to concentrate. And you didn't even care about my safety," she retorted, her voice shaking with a mix of fear and fury.

Ross's eyes narrowed, his tone dripping with disdain. "You don't get to make excuses, Maria. Fix it."

Suppressing her frustration, Maria left the office and went back to the warehouse. However, the pressure of the day and the looming danger were overwhelming. She stopped and took a deep breath, realizing she couldn't finish the count accurately under these conditions. The mounting stress and Ross's dismissive attitude had pushed her to her breaking point.

Suppressing her frustration, Maria decided to leave the warehouse without completing the count. She felt a wave of exhaustion and anger wash over her as she walked out. She couldn't take Ross's treatment any longer. Her safety, her dignity, and her peace of mind were more important than this job.

She pulled out her phone and typed a message to Ross: "I quit."

With that decisive action, she knew there was no turning back. She immediately texted Franz: "Can you pick me up? I'm at the warehouse."

Franz responded almost immediately: "On my way. Are you okay?"

Maria took a deep breath and replied, "I'll explain when you get here."

As she waited, the enormity of her decision began to sink in. Quitting her job was a huge step into the unknown, but Ross's relentless mistreatment had left her with no choice. She felt a mix of fear and relief, knowing that she had taken a stand for herself.

When Franz arrived, his face was etched with concern. "Maria, what happened?" he asked as she got into the car.

Maria looked out the window, gathering her thoughts. "I quit my job today," she said quietly. "Ross pushed me too far. He didn't care about my safety and treated me horribly. I couldn't take it anymore."

Maria looked out the window, gathering her thoughts. She continued to tell Franz the details of what had happened—the threats, the unsafe work conditions, Ross's cruel jokes, and the final straw that had led her to walk away. Franz listened intently, his grip on the steering wheel tightening with each word.

As she recounted the events, Franz's jaw clenched. He took a deep breath, trying to contain his anger. It was clear he was furious, but he remained focused on Maria, offering her the support she desperately needed.

When she finished, he glanced at her, his eyes softening. "We'll figure it out. You're not alone in this. And I'm proud of you for standing up for yourself."

Maria sighed, a mix of relief and frustration washing over her. "I know. But it's still hard to walk away, especially without a plan."

Franz reached over and gave her hand a reassuring squeeze. "We'll get through this together," he said firmly. "One step at a time."

Maria managed a small smile, grateful for his support. As they drove away from town, she felt a glimmer of hope amidst the uncertainty, knowing that she wasn't facing this challenge alone.

Chapter 19: Echoes of Resilience

Maria finished packing her belongings, bidding farewell to her housemates, particularly Heidi. "I'll miss our weekend gym sessions," she said, embracing her friend. "But we'll still see each other there, right?"

Heidi nodded, returning the hug. "Of course! And don't forget to message us when you settle into your new place. We'll have to celebrate your new beginnings!"

As Maria exchanged farewells with John, Alex, and Jean, they expressed their support. "You've got this, Maria," Jean said, giving her a reassuring smile. "We'll keep in touch and wait for your updates."

As she left her old apartment behind, Maria moved into Franz's place, grateful for his unwavering support in the aftermath of her resignation. Franz had been her rock, providing comfort and stability during a tumultuous time.

Meanwhile, the Kapampangan community rallied around Maria, expressing their desire to escalate the matter with Ross's treatment. However, both the company and the association came to an agreement not to cancel Maria's work visa until she found a new job, ensuring she could stay in Lae.

"Thank you for everything, Franz," Maria said, her voice filled with emotion as they settled into their new routine. "I don't know what I would do without you."

Franz smiled, squeezing her hand gently. "You don't have to thank me. I'm just glad I can be here for you."

Throughout the evening, Maria and Franz talked late into the night, sharing stories of their past. And as Maria drifted off to sleep, she felt a sense of peace settle over her, knowing that no matter what challenges lay ahead, she had friends who would always have her back.

In the morning, Franz wasted no time in reaching out to his boss about the possibility of hiring Maria as an office manager. He believed in her abilities and was determined to help her find a new path forward.

Chapter 20: Waiting for Tomorrow

The morning sun filtered through the curtains as Maria stirred awake to Franz's gentle kisses. They had been together for a month now, their bond growing stronger each day.

"Good morning, my love," Franz whispered, his voice filled with warmth.

"Good morning," Maria replied, smiling softly.

As they shared breakfast, Maria couldn't shake off her worries about her job situation. It had been six weeks since Franz messaged her boss about a job for her, yet there was still no progress. "Any news from your boss about the job?" she asked, concern lacing her voice.

Franz sighed, shaking his head. "Not yet, but I'm hopeful. Ruby just needs to finish her notice period, and then you'll start working."

Maria nodded, trying to stay positive. "I hope it's soon. I miss having a routine and contributing financially."

"Don't worry about that," Franz reassured her, squeezing her hand. "I'll take care of us until then."

Maria felt a surge of gratitude towards Franz for his unwavering support. "Thank you, Franz. I appreciate everything you do for me."

As they went about their day, Maria found joy in the simple tasks of homemaking. She cooked meals for Franz, cleaned the house, and tended to their needs. Despite the uncertainty, she relished in the role of a supportive partner.

In the evenings, Maria would often reflect on her family and the secrets she kept from them. She had told them about her relationship with Franz but omitted the live-in arrangement, fearing their disapproval. She also chose not to disclose her resignation. The guilt weighed heavily on her heart, but she hoped that once she found new employment, she could finally reveal her job situation.

With each passing day, Maria found herself counting down the moments until she could share her news with her family and embark on the next chapter of her life.

Chapter 21: Draft Night Discoveries: Nostalgia, Betrayal, and Unforeseen Turns

Franz, Maria, Arnold, and Denise gathered around a table at the Lae City Hotel's restaurant, their excitement palpable as they discussed the upcoming basketball draft over plates of seafood and glasses of beer and cocktails. As the ones in charge of the draft, they were eager to see which new players would join the league.

"I heard there are some amazing rookies this season," Maria said, her eyes shining with excitement. "I'm so stoked!"

Franz nodded in agreement. "Yeah, I've heard rumors about some incredible talent. We should make sure to get it right."

As they continued to chat, Denise turned to Maria and asked, "So, when can we expect you to start at your new job?"

Maria's face lit up. "Ruby is finishing serving her notice today, so I'm hoping to start next week."

Arnold spoke up. "That's great news! I'm sure you'll do a great job, Maria."

Denise nodded in agreement. "Yeah, I'm sure you will too."

The conversation continued, with Maria and Franz discussing their plans for the upcoming weeks. Denise was happy to see them so happy and content in their relationship.

As they wrapped up the meeting, Maria got up to grab another drink. "Hey, guys, I'll be right back."

Franz nodded and turned back to Arnold. "So, what do you think of the new rookies?"

Arnold shrugged. "I think they have potential. But we'll have to see how they perform in the draft."

Franz nodded in agreement. "Yeah, it's always exciting to see new talent emerge."

As Maria returned with her drink, Denise smiled at the couple. "You know, I'm really happy for you two. You're great together."

Maria blushed and smiled at Franz. "Thanks, Denise. We're very happy too."

As the afternoon waned, Franz approached Maria, requesting her to draft a summary of potential draft players. As she diligently typed away, her fingers dancing over the keys, she felt a pang in her chest as her eyes landed on a name etched in her memory. The mere sight of it unleashed a flood of emotions within her, dredging up memories of a love once cherished but now tainted by betrayal and abandonment. Despite the warmth of Franz's presence beside her, Maria couldn't shake off the haunting specter of her past love. With each keystroke, she found herself engulfed in a whirlwind of conflicting feelings, torn between the affection she held for Franz and the unresolved emotions tied to her past. And there it was, glaring back at her from the screen: Dean Aquino.

Maria's heart clenched in disbelief as she stared at the screen. Could it be? She desperately hoped it was a different Dean Aquino, not the one etched into her memories with pain.

But as she grappled with her thoughts, Franz's voice sliced through her turmoil. "Hey, ready to go? April's birthday bash awaits."

With a nod, Maria tried to shake off her unease. Yet, as they stepped into the festivities, a cold shiver ran down her spine at the sight of an unfamiliar car parked outside. Suddenly, April, the birthday host and Jun's girlfriend, seized the microphone, her voice ringing with excitement as she introduced a new addition to their Kapampangan community: Dean.

Maria's heart plummeted like a stone as the truth dawned upon her—indeed, it was him... *her Dean.*

Maria's heart raced, her complexion paling, but she prayed no one would notice. As everyone was introduced and shook hands with Dean, when it was her turn, she stammered, "Hi, Dean." Dean's demeanor remained composed, as if nothing had transpired.

After the introduction, Dean seemed to act as if he hadn't met Maria before, seamlessly continuing the conversation. As they talked, Maria learned that Dean had resigned due to a job opportunity in Wewak, now assigned to Lae. But why hadn't he contacted her?

She couldn't shake off her confusion, especially after discovering he'd been separated for months now. Despite searching for any sign of remorse or guilt on his face, she found none.

Suddenly, someone emerged from Dean's car, having fallen asleep inside. It was a woman. Dean approached her and led her to the group. "Everyone, meet Princess. My girlfriend."

Chapter 22: Crossroads at the Fuel Company

Maria's alarm buzzed early, but she was already awake, excitement and nerves mingling as she prepared for her first day as the office manager at the fuel company. She chose her outfit carefully, hoping to make a good impression, and as the morning light filtered through their apartment, Franz kissed her on the cheek.

"You're going to be amazing today," he assured her, his voice filled with confidence and affection.

"Thanks, Franz," Maria replied, squeezing his hand. "I'm just a bit nervous, but I'm really looking forward to it."

As they walked to the office together, the warm sun reflected off the quiet streets of Lae. The small team greeted them with friendly smiles. It was a modest operation, but Maria felt a surge of optimism. Franz, already familiar with the team, introduced her around with pride.

"Mama! Papa!" Maria greeted them with enthusiasm, her voice filled with warmth. Two days had passed since Maria confided in her parents about her new job and the turmoil she faced at her previous one. The sense of relief she felt was overwhelming.

"Maria! How was your first day?" her mother asked, her voice tinged with both curiosity and relief.

Maria's face brightened. "It was wonderful, Mama. The team is great, and the office feels like a perfect fit for me. Everything seems to be falling into place."

Her father's eyes shone with pride. "We're so proud of you, *anak*. We knew you would excel."

They chatted about her new role, the company, and how she was settling into life in Lae. Her parents' encouragement and love wrapped around her like a comforting blanket, making the distance between them seem a little less vast.

The following week, Maria noticed Franz and Dean talking animatedly in the office lounge. They seemed to have struck up a friendship, their laughter echoing through the corridors. It was odd, seeing Dean in her workplace, so integrated into her present life while still being a part of her past.

Franz caught her eye and waved her over. "Maria, come join us. Dean was just sharing some interesting insights about our upcoming projects."

Dean turned to her with a nod and a professional smile. "Maria, it's good to see you. We were discussing the logistics for the new fuel supply chain. Your input could be valuable."

As they delved into the conversation, Maria couldn't help but marvel at the strange twists of fate. Here she was, working alongside Franz, her supportive partner, while Dean, her past love, was evolving into a pivotal figure and developing a close friendship with Franz within their professional realm.

In the following days, Maria adeptly balanced her duties with a growing sense of assurance. Yet, during moments of solitude, she found herself pondering Dean's presence. His composed demeanor at the party, his newfound relationship, and his budding friendship with Franz stirred a whirlwind of emotions within her.

She couldn't shake off the nagging questions about why Dean hadn't reached out to her during his separation. Did he easily forget their shared past? Or was there more complexity beneath the surface? Despite her resolve to focus on her current job and life, these lingering uncertainties persisted, casting shadows on her thoughts.

Amidst her contemplation, Maria also found herself pondering about Princess, Dean's new girlfriend. Although they had briefly met at the party and Princess seemed amiable, Maria couldn't help but wonder about the intricacies of their relationship. The thought of Dean swiftly moving on added an additional layer of complexity to Maria's emotions.

Despite knowing she shouldn't dwell on it, Maria found herself unable to completely set aside these thoughts. She was committed to Franz, and their relationship was a source of strength and happiness. Yet, the unresolved feelings and unanswered questions from her past continued to tug at her conscience.

As Maria traversed through this new phase of her life, she stood at a crossroads, with the future holding both promise and uncertainty. The intertwining of her past and present created a complex mosaic of relationships, career aspirations, and personal introspection. Amidst it all, Maria grappled with the realization that she should feel anger or resentment towards the man who had betrayed her. However, despite her efforts, she couldn't muster any of those emotions, leaving her feeling unsettled and confused.

Moreover, Maria found herself torn between the urge to confide in Franz about her past with Dean and the fear of jeopardizing their relationship. She weighed the consequences of revealing such intimate details against the potential strain it could place on their bond, unsure of which path to choose.

Chapter 23: Resurfacing Echoes

Maria had outdone herself for Franz's birthday party, transforming their apartment into a vibrant celebration of Filipino culture. The room was adorned with colorful streamers and balloons in red, blue, and yellow, the colors of the Filipino flag. The long table was laden with an array of Filipino delicacies—*lechon, pancit, menudo*, and other mouthwatering dishes. The familiar aromas filled the air, creating a warm, inviting atmosphere.

"Maria, this is incredible," Denise exclaimed as she arrived, taking in the festive decorations.

"Thank you, Denise," Maria responded with a radiant smile. "I wanted to make it special for Franz."

Soon, the apartment buzzed with guests: the Pampanga Dragons, Denise, Arnold, Dean, and Heidi. Dean's girlfriend, Princess, couldn't make it because she was feeling under the weather. Laughter and animated chatter filled the room as friends helped themselves to the feast and settled in for an evening of fun and camaraderie.

As the night wore on, the beer flowed freely, and the karaoke machine was put to good use. Dean's deep voice boomed through the speakers, and Maria, Denise, and Heidi joined in, their voices mingling with the music and laughter.

Franz, with a bottle of beer in hand and a rosy flush spreading across his cheeks, joined the Pampanga Dragons in a spirited discussion about their next basketball game.

"We need to tighten our defense," Arnold suggested, leaning forward with a serious expression. "Last game, we were all over the place."

Franz nodded, his speech slightly slurred. "Yeah, but if we can get our offense aligned... we'll dominate."

Jun, another team member, chimed in, "Exactly! We need better communication on the court. It's not just about skill; it's about how we play as a team."

Franz nodded again, trying to keep his focus. "Yes... and we need to pace ourselves. Let's not burn out too early."

Denise, Heidi, and Maria had their own lively conversation about their plans for their next badminton session.

"We should try doubles next time,' Heidi suggested. "It's more fun and definitely more challenging."

"Absolutely!" Maria agreed. "Plus, it's a great way to bond and strategize."

Throughout the evening, Maria couldn't help but notice Dean's interactions. Unlike the previous gathering where he pretended not to know her, tonight, he seemed more open and relaxed. He laughed with friends, joined in the karaoke, and engaged in conversations, acknowledging Maria naturally, as if their shared past was no longer a secret or a burden. Yet, whenever their eyes met, there was an unspoken tension, a connection that they both seemed to skirt around.

As the night progressed, Franz's speech became more slurred, and his steps more unsteady. Guests started to leave, each thanking Maria and Franz for the wonderful evening.

"Great party, Maria," one of the Pampanga Dragons said as he headed out. "Thanks for having us!"

"Anytime!" Maria replied warmly, waving goodbye.

By the end of the night, only Denise, Arnold, and Dean remained. They stayed behind to help Maria with the cleanup while Franz, clearly inebriated, slouched on the couch, mumbling incoherently.

"Didn't know Franz could handle his beer this well," Arnold joked, carefully stacking the plates.

"He's usually not like this," Maria said, half-laughing, half-worried as she looked at Franz, who was now muttering about basketball and their next game.

114

"We'll help you get him to bed," Dean offered. Together, they managed to guide Franz to the bedroom. He collapsed onto the bed, still mumbling, before drifting off.

With Franz safely in bed, Maria returned to the living room to finish tidying up with the others.

"You really went all out tonight, Maria," Denise said as she picked up some empty bottles. "Franz is lucky to have you."

Maria smiled, though her thoughts were a tangle of worry and affection. "Thank you, Denise. I just wanted everyone to have a good time."

Denise and Arnold soon gathered their things, preparing to leave. "We should get going," Arnold said, glancing at the clock. "It's late."

"Thanks so much for your help," Maria said, hugging them both. "I really appreciate it."

"No problem at all. Get some rest," Denise replied with a knowing smile. "And good luck with Franz when he wakes up."

Maria chuckled, "I'll need it."

As the door closed behind Denise and Arnold, Maria turned around to find herself alone with Dean. The remnants of the evening's festivities lingered in the air, and an awkward silence settled between them.

Dean cleared his throat, breaking the silence. "That was a great party, Maria. You did an amazing job."

"Thank you," Maria replied, her voice tinged with uncertainty. "I just wanted to make sure everyone had a good time."

They stood there for a moment, the weight of their shared past hanging between them. It was surreal to be in this intimate setting with Dean after so long, especially with Franz asleep in the next room.

Dean finally spoke, his voice soft and tentative. "It's strange, isn't it? Being here like this, after everything."

Maria's eyes narrowed slightly. "Yes, it is. Considering you acted like you didn't even know me the last time we met."

Dean looked down, guilt and regret shadowing his face. "I'm sorry for that. I didn't know how to handle seeing you again."

Maria's voice took on a sharp edge. "You mean seeing me again and pretending we had no history? Or seeing me again after keeping the fact that you were married from me?"

Dean winced at her words but met her gaze steadily. "You have every right to be angry, Maria. I was a coward back then. But I never meant to hurt you."

Maria let out a bitter laugh, shaking her head. "Never meant to hurt me? Dean, you vanished without a word. Not even a call. And all this time, I've been beating myself up, thinking I was responsible for wrecking your family."

Dean stepped closer, his expression earnest. "Maria, it wasn't your fault. When we met, my marriage was already over. We were just going through the motions, waiting for the inevitable. I was on the verge of separation."

Maria's breath hitched at his words. She had carried the guilt and pain of their affair, believing she had been the cause of a broken family. Hearing this truth felt like a weight lifting off her shoulders, a breath of fresh air after being submerged in guilt for so long. Yet, the relief was tangled with sadness and unresolved emotions.

"But why didn't you tell me?" she asked, her voice softer now, tinged with the vulnerability she had tried so hard to suppress.

Dean sighed, rubbing the back of his neck. "I was ashamed. Ashamed of my failing marriage, ashamed of dragging you into my mess. And when I got the job in Wewak, I thought it was a chance to start over, to escape."

Maria looked away, blinking back tears. "You could have trusted me, Dean. We could have figured it out together."

Dean reached out as if to touch her arm but stopped himself. "I know. I'm sorry. Truly. I just... didn't know how."

They stood in silence, the room filled with the echoes of unspoken words and missed opportunities. Maria felt a swirl of emotions—relief, sadness, and a bittersweet acceptance. She had loved Dean deeply, and while that love had been tainted by secrets and betrayal, it had also been real and profound.

"I'm with Franz now," she said finally, her voice steady. "And you have Princess. We've both moved on."

Dean nodded, a faint, rueful smile on his lips. "I'm glad you found happiness, Maria. You deserve it."

Maria managed a small, tentative smile in return. "Thank you. I hope you find it too."

Dean's expression softened, his eyes reflecting a mixture of regret and acceptance. "For what it's worth, I am sorry. I should have been honest with you from the start."

Maria nodded, the tension in her chest easing slightly. "I appreciate that, Dean. And I'm sorry too... for everything."

Dean shook his head gently. "You have nothing to apologize for. It was never your fault."

As he spoke, Maria felt a heavy weight lift off her shoulders. The guilt she had carried for so long seemed to dissolve, replaced by a sense of closure and clarity.

With that, Dean turned and headed towards the door. "Good night, Maria. Take care."

"Good night, Dean," she replied softly as he stepped out into the cool night air.

As the door clicked shut, Maria leaned against it, taking a deep breath. The evening had been a success, but now, with Franz asleep and the guests gone, she was left alone with her thoughts— and the strange sense of closure that Dean's confession had brought.

Chapter 24: No More Secrets

Maria looked for a quiet place to call her parents. She found solace in the backyard, a small haven of tranquility amidst her swirling thoughts. The weight of unspoken truths was pressing down on her, and she knew it was time to come clean. She needed to tell them everything—the live-in arrangement with Franz, her supportive partner, and the unexpected reconnection with Dean. The guilt was becoming unbearable.

With a deep breath, Maria dialed their number.

"Hi, Mama. Hi, Papa," Maria began, her voice trembling slightly. "I need to talk to you about something important."

"Maria, what's wrong?" her mother asked, concern evident in her tone.

Maria swallowed hard. "It's about my living situation... and Dean," she continued, forcing herself to stay calm. "Franz and I have been living together for some time now. And there's something else—I need to tell you that Dean is in Lae too. We've met again, and he's becoming an important part of our lives, especially for Franz. I haven't told you this before because I was afraid of how you'd react."

There was a long, heavy silence before her father's voice broke through, stern and disapproving. "You mean to say you're living with Franz and that Dean is involved in your lives now? Maria, what are you thinking?"

Maria braced herself, feeling the weight of their disappointment. "Yes, Papa. Franz and I are living together. Dean and I have reconnected, and he's become a close friend to Franz. It all happened so unexpectedly, but it's the truth."

Her parents had always been a pillar of unwavering Catholic faith and conservative values. Their lives were shaped by traditions and beliefs that left little room for deviation. Maria had known from the beginning that this conversation would be difficult. She had grown up in a household where the sanctity of marriage and the adherence to religious norms were paramount. Living with someone outside of marriage was almost unthinkable, and reconnecting with a past love added layers of complexity that she knew they would struggle to understand.

Her mother's voice softened, tinged with sadness and confusion. "Maria, you know we love you. But this... this isn't right. Our beliefs, our values—they've always guided us. How could you keep this from us?"

"Mama, Papa," Maria said, her voice catching in her throat, "I know this isn't what you expected. I've always respected our family's values, but I'm old enough to make my own decisions. This is my life, and I'm happy with how things are. Franz has been incredibly supportive, and reconnecting with Dean has brought a sense of closure and new beginnings. I need you to understand that."

Her father's tone hardened, filled with a mix of disappointment and anger. "We raised you with certain values, Maria. This... this isn't what we expected from you. We just want you to come home. To be with your family, where you belong."

Maria's heart ached with the weight of their expectations. "I can't do that, Papa. I have to keep moving forward on my own path. I need to find my own way."

The conversation ended with her parents feeling hurt and angry, their voices echoing in her mind. The knot in Maria's stomach tightened. Had she done enough to deserve their understanding? Did her choices make her a bad daughter? The questions gnawed at her, each one heavier than the last.

As she stood there, lost in these troubling thoughts, Maria turned around. Her heart skipped a beat as she realized someone had been listening.

Franz.

Chapter 25: Shattered Trust

Maria's confession hung heavy in the air as Franz processed the revelation. His emotions swirled like a tempest within him, hurt and betrayal clouding his thoughts.

"What do you mean you had a relationship with Dean without telling me?" Franz's voice trembled with a mix of hurt and anger.

Maria's heart sank. "Franz, please," she implored, her voice quivering with emotion. "Dean and I have a history, something from before you and I were together. I didn't know how to tell you. I didn't want to hurt you."

"Hurt me?" Franz's voice thundered, the anger palpable in the room. "You've made a fool out of me! You and Dean! How could you keep something like this from me?"

Tears welled in Maria's eyes as she struggled to explain. "I'm so sorry, Franz. I should have told you sooner. But Dean and I are just friends now, nothing more. I didn't mean to betray your trust."

But Franz's rage knew no bounds. "You won't see Dean again. If you want this relationship to work, you have to avoid any interaction with him."

"Franz, please," Maria pleaded, desperation lacing her words. "Dean is a part of my past."

"You brought this on yourself," Franz spat, his voice dripping with venom. "I trusted you, Maria. And now you've broken that trust. You will follow my rules, or there will be no relationship."

He turned away, his back rigid with anger. "I'll tell the security to keep an eye on you. Apart from work, you're not going anywhere else without my permission."

Maria protested, her voice tinged with disbelief. "But Franz, that's not fair! I can't be restricted like this!"

Franz interrupted, his tone uncompromising. "It's for the best, Maria. You've broken my trust, and I need to know where you are at all times."

Maria's heart shattered as Franz's words pierced her soul. "What have I done?" she whispered to herself, her spirit crushed beneath the weight of her mistakes. "I've destroyed everything."

Franz's words cut through her like a knife. "You have no one to blame but yourself. You kept secrets from me. You lied to us."

With her relationship with her family already on the brink, Maria felt her world crumbling. She had thought she was doing the right thing by being honest with her parents, but that had only driven a wedge between them. And now, with Franz's trust shattered, she was losing him too.

"I can't believe you would do this to me," Franz said, his voice quieter now, but no less angry. "I thought we had something real, something strong. But you've ruined it."

Maria's sobs were the only sound in the room as Franz turned his back on her, leaving her to grapple with the wreckage of their relationship. She had never felt so alone, so isolated. The life she had built was once again falling apart, and she didn't know how to fix it.

As the night wore on, Maria sat alone, contemplating the ruins of her choices. It had been a while since she last prayed, truly and sincerely. She had forgotten God in the chaos of her life, but now she needed Him the most. With a heavy heart and tear-streaked face, Maria bowed her head and began to pray, seeking solace and guidance in the midst of her shattered trust and broken dreams.

Chapter 26: Fractured Bonds

The silence in the dining room was broken only by the clinking of Franz's fork against his plate. He speared a piece of chicken but left it untouched, his gaze fixed on a point somewhere beyond the window. Maria sat across from him, her back ramrod straight, a stark contrast to her usual relaxed posture during meals.

"Franz," Maria started cautiously, her voice laced with a tremor that betrayed her attempt at composure. "We need to have a conversation about this."

Franz sighed, a heavy sound that seemed to steal the air from the room. "About what, Maria?" he mumbled, not meeting her eyes.

"About everything," she said, her voice firm despite the slight wobble in her lips. "About the way you've been acting lately, the distance you've put between us and everyone else."

He finally looked up, his expression guarded. "It's not about you," he mumbled defensively.

"Don't insult my intelligence, Franz," she countered, a spark of defiance igniting in her eyes. "You've practically forbidden me from seeing Arnold, Denise, even Heidi. What is it you're so afraid of?"

"Forbidden isn't the right word," he mumbled, avoiding her gaze. "I just… I don't know if it's a good idea for you to be around them right now."

"Why not?" she pressed, her voice laced with concern.

"It's just a feeling," he admitted, his voice laced with frustration. "A feeling that maybe they know something about your past with Dean, something they haven't told me."

The color drained from Maria's face for a moment, then a flicker of anger replaced it. "So that's it," she said, her voice tight. "You think my friends are hiding things from you?"

"I don't know," he confessed, his voice dropping to a whisper. "It just… bothers me that they haven't mentioned it. Makes me wonder what else they might be keeping secret."

Maria shook her head, tears welling in her eyes. "Franz, Dean is in the past. Those people are my friends, and they've never done anything to hurt us."

"Friends who keep secrets?" he shot back, his voice laced with suspicion.

"Secrets that don't concern you, Franz!" she cried, her voice rising with each word. "This isn't about them, it's about you and your insecurities!"

The anger in her voice fueled his own. "Maybe you're right," he said, his voice hardening. "Maybe I am insecure! But can you blame me? You haven't exactly been forthcoming about your past!"

"I've already explained everything countless times, Franz! What else do you want to hear?" she cried, slamming her hands on the table, the clatter echoing in the tense silence.

"It's not enough!" he roared, his voice cracking with a mixture of anger and hurt. "Not when it feels like everyone is hiding something from me!"

The room spun for a moment as a searing pain erupted across Maria's cheek. Franz's hand hung suspended in the air, the echo of the slap hanging heavy in the thick silence. Maria's hand flew to her face, tears streaming down now.

Shame and regret flooded Franz's face as the weight of his action hit him. He reached out for her, but she flinched away, her eyes filled with a mixture of anger and a deep betrayal that cut him to the core.

"Get out," she whispered, her voice choked with emotion. "Just... get out."

Franz stood there, frozen, the remnants of their shattered dinner scattered around him like a metaphor for their fractured bond.

He turned and walked out, leaving Maria alone in the wreckage of their trust.

Chapter 27: Wings Unfurled

Maria had been plotting her escape for days. A well-practiced cough and a mumbled excuse about a stomach ache sent Franz off to work, blissfully unaware of the storm brewing in his absence. The moment the door clicked shut, Maria sprang into action. Clothes, essentials, her passport—each item a brick in the wall she was building between her old life and the new one beckoning. The one-way ticket to the Philippines felt heavy in her hand, a tangible symbol of her liberation.

Time was a predator at her heels. Maria had already secretly arranged for Dean's help, a strange twist of fate considering their past. Despite the tangled history, he'd become her lifeline when she confessed the suffocating reality of her life with Franz. Their rendezvous point was set. To ensure no interruptions, she told the security guard she needed medicine for a stomach ache and requested him to buy some medicine. She asked him to leave it on the dining table while she rested.

The rumble of Dean's engine sent a jolt through her. Relief and a tremor of fear warred within her as she darted out of the house and into the waiting car. The city blurred past as they sped towards the airport, a whirlwind of emotions swirling in her gut.

"Thank you for this, Dean," she said, her voice barely a whisper.

Dean didn't meet her gaze. "It's the least I can do," he muttered, his jaw clenched.

Maria knew there was more he wanted to say, apologies bubbling under the surface. She didn't need them. Not anymore. The past was a burden she was finally shedding.

As they neared the airport, a steely resolve settled in her eyes. "I can't live like that anymore," she declared, her voice firm. "I deserve better. This... this is for me."

Dean nodded, a flicker of something akin to admiration crossing his features. "You absolutely do, Maria. Go be happy."

At the terminal, a bittersweet goodbye unfolded. Maria handed Dean a stack of carefully worded letters. "These are thank you notes for my friends," she explained, her voice tight with emotion. "I wrote a little about the emergency situation at home."

"Emergency?" Dean raised an eyebrow. "Everything alright?"

"I'll explain when I can." Maria hedged, avoiding specifics. "And if Franz reaches out to any of them..."

Dean cut her off, a confident smirk playing on his lips. "Don't worry about that. I'll handle things here. You focus on starting fresh."

Maria searched his eyes, a silent question hanging in the air.

"Starting over isn't ideal," he continued, his voice softening. "But you're strong, Maria. You've faced worse. This time, you'll do it right. You'll build a life that truly makes you happy."

A surge of determination washed over Maria. She wasn't afraid to begin again. This time, the pieces she built would be her own, a testament to her resilience.

"Thank you, Dean," she whispered, the words thick with gratitude. "For everything."

The terminal buzzed with activity, a stark contrast to the quiet resolve simmering within Maria. With a final goodbye to Dean, she clutched the boarding pass, a ticket to a future she'd design on her own terms. A resolute click on her phone confirmed what she'd already done- Franz was blocked. Every avenue of communication severed, a symbolic act mirroring the wall she'd built around her heart. The Philippines, her homeland, awaited. Not a place to hide, but a new blank canvas, a chance to rewrite her story.

Part of her had considered staying, finding another job, maybe even applying for work abroad. But a deeper truth gnawed at her. The cracks in her foundation weren't just about Franz; they were about the wounded relationship with her family. She couldn't keep running, couldn't keep building a life on shaky ground. This trip wasn't just an escape, it was a chance to reconnect, to heal the wounds that had festered for too long. She wouldn't allow the past to dictate her future. This time, armed with hard-won lessons and a fierce determination, she would ensure every brushstroke nourished the life she craved—a life brimming with self-respect, happiness, and the unwavering belief that she deserved it all. As she boarded the plane, a single tear traced a path down her cheek, not one of sorrow, but a glistening promise—a promise to paint a masterpiece. This time, she wouldn't settle for anything less.

Chapter 28: Homecoming Tears

Maria's hands trembled as the plane descended, her heart pounding with anticipation. This was it—she was almost home. The small, familiar town of Santa Ana came into view as the plane touched down. It was still early, the sun just beginning to cast its warm glow over the sleepy streets. Her eyes welled up with tears of relief and excitement. She was back, back to where it all began, to the place she had longed for in her most vulnerable moments.

She quickly collected her belongings and stepped out of the airport, taking in the vibrant yet serene atmosphere of the town. The narrow streets buzzed with life as people started their day, greeting each other with warm smiles and familiar nods. Santa Ana was a small town, rich in tradition and community spirit, a place where everyone knew each other and life's pace was gentle.

Flagging down a tricycle, she felt a wave of nostalgia. The rickety vehicle brought back memories of her childhood, of simpler times. She chatted briefly with the driver, who was delighted to hear about her return after a long time away. As they wove through the town's narrow lanes, Maria soaked in every detail—the vendors setting up their stalls, the children playing in the streets, the church bells chiming in the distance. The ride felt both liberating and grounding, reconnecting her with the roots she had missed so dearly.

Arriving at her family's house just as the clock struck eight, Maria's breath caught in her throat. There, on the terrace, sat her father, his face partly hidden behind a newspaper. He was a picture of calm, completely unaware of the emotional storm about to hit him.

"Papa!" Maria called out, her voice cracking with a mix of joy and sorrow.

Her father looked up, his eyes widening in disbelief as he recognized his daughter. "Maria?" he whispered, the newspaper slipping from his grasp.

In a flash, Maria was out of the tricycle and running towards him. As they embraced, months of pent-up emotions broke free. Maria clung to her father, sobbing uncontrollably. The sheer relief of being in his protective arms was overwhelming.

"Papa, I'm so sorry," Maria cried, her voice muffled against his shoulder. "I've missed you so much. I've been such a fool."

Her father held her tight, his own eyes glistening with tears. "You're home now, Maria. That's all that matters. You're safe here."

Just then, her younger sister Lucy appeared at the door, her eyes widening in shock. "Ma! *Ate* is here!" she shouted, her voice ringing with excitement.

In moments, her mother and younger brother Miguel rushed out, their faces lighting up with joy and relief. Maria found herself enveloped in a family hug, each of them holding on as if they would never let go.

"Mama, I'm sorry," Maria sobbed, burying her face in her mother's shoulder. "You and Papa were right. I shouldn't have moved in with Franz. I should have respected myself more. I should have taken more time to get to know him. He turned into a monster, and I didn't see it coming."

Her mother stroked her hair, her voice soothing and warm. "Hush, *anak*. You're home now. We're here for you, and no one can hurt you anymore. Welcome home, my dear."

Miguel, hugging her from the side, chimed in, "Yeah, *Ate*. We've got your back."

Maria's father, holding her close, added, "We all make mistakes, Maria. What's important is that you're back with us, where you belong. We love you, and we'll get through this together."

As they stood there, entwined in each other's embrace, Maria felt a profound sense of peace. The guilt and shame that had weighed her down were slowly lifting. She was home, surrounded by the people who loved her unconditionally. They were her strength, her refuge, and in their arms, she found the courage to face the future anew.

The morning air was crisp, carrying the scent of flowers and freshly brewed coffee from nearby houses. As Maria looked around, she realized that this was where she was meant to be—with her family, in Santa Ana, starting over and reclaiming her life. The path ahead was uncertain, but she was ready to face it, knowing that she had the unwavering support of her loved ones.

In this small, vibrant town, Maria found not just a place, but a purpose. She was ready to build a new life, one step at a time, surrounded by the warmth and love that only home could provide.

Chapter 29: Embracing New Paths

Maria and her friend Chu sat across from each other at their favorite local diner, their faces glowing with the soft, ambient light. The hum of conversation, clinking utensils, and the aroma of sizzling dishes created a comforting backdrop. For Maria, being here with Chu felt like coming home.

"I can't believe you're really back," Chu said, her eyes sparkling as she took a sip of her iced tea. "I've missed you so much. Facebook chats just weren't the same."

Maria smiled, feeling a warmth spread through her chest. "I know, Chu. I missed you too. Those messages were a lifeline for me. It feels surreal to be sitting here with you."

Chu nodded, her expression shifting to one of concern. "How are you holding up? I know you've been through a lot more than our chats could cover."

Maria took a deep breath, the weight of her past months hanging in the air. "I'm... better. Being home, surrounded by family and friends, it's been healing. I finally closed that chapter of my life with Franz. It was hard, but necessary. I'm ready to start over and build something new."

Chu reached across the table, giving Maria's hand a reassuring squeeze. "I'm so proud of you. You've been through so much, and yet here you are, standing strong."

Maria's eyes welled up with tears, but she blinked them away, grateful for Chu's unwavering support. "Thank you. I couldn't have done it without you and everyone here. And you know what? I realized how much I missed teaching. There's something so fulfilling about being in the classroom."

Chu's face lit up with excitement. "That's perfect timing because St. Michael's is looking for a math teacher for next school year. With your history there, I bet you'll get the job easily."

Maria's heart skipped a beat. "Are you serious? That would be amazing. I've always loved teaching there. I'll definitely apply."

That evening, Maria sat at her laptop, her fingers flying over the keyboard as she poured her heart into her cover letter and resume. She wanted to convey her passion for teaching and her readiness to embrace this new chapter. Once satisfied, she hit send and leaned back, a mix of hope and anticipation swirling inside her.

The following morning, her phone pinged with a new email notification. Her eyes widened as she read the message from St. Michael's. They wanted her for an interview and a lesson presentation.

"They responded so quickly!" Maria exclaimed to Chu over the phone. "They want me to come in for an interview and to present a lesson. You didn't mention there's a new principal."

"Oh, right!" Chu laughed. "Ms. Santos is new, but she's wonderful. She's really been shaking things up in a good way. And don't worry, Maria, I've told her all about your amazing teaching skills."

Maria felt a surge of gratitude for Chu. "Thank you. It means a lot to have your support."

Later that day, Maria dressed in her best professional attire and made her way to St. Michael's Catholic School. Walking through the familiar hallways, memories flooded back, filling her with both nostalgia and determination.

The interview with Ms. Santos went smoothly. She was warm and welcoming, and her smile eased Maria's nerves. "I've heard wonderful things about you, Maria," she said. "Your passion for teaching and your rapport with the students are exactly what we're looking for."

Maria's heart swelled with pride and relief. "Thank you, Ms. Santos. St. Michael's has always been special to me. I'd be honored to return."

After the interview, Maria stood in front of a classroom, presenting her lesson to a room full of attentive students. The familiar rhythm of teaching brought a smile to her face. By the end of the day, she received the call she had been hoping for.

"We'd love to have you join our team," Ms. Santos said warmly. "Welcome back to St. Michael's, Maria."

Maria hung up the phone, tears of joy streaming down her face. She had done it. She was finally home, ready to start anew, embracing the bright future ahead.

Chapter 30: A Season of Celebration

Maria stood at the front of the conference room, adjourning the meeting with her co-curricular team. The energy in the room was palpable, a mix of excitement and anticipation as they finalized plans for the upcoming Gratitude Day celebration. It was the biggest event of the year, a day when the entire St. Michael's Catholic School community—students, teachers, non-teaching staff, and parents—came together to celebrate with vibrant dance presentations and festivities.

"Thank you, everyone, for your hard work and dedication," Maria said, her voice warm and encouraging. "Gratitude Day is our chance to showcase the spirit and unity of our school. Let's make this year's celebration the best one yet!"

The team members smiled and nodded, their faces reflecting a shared sense of purpose. This would be Maria's fifth time leading the event, including her previous years at St. Michael's. Her experience and passion made her the natural choice for the role of co-curricular coordinator, a position she cherished deeply.

As the team dispersed, Maria remained behind for a moment, her eyes sweeping over the detailed plans and schedules pinned on the board. She meticulously reviewed each element, ensuring that no detail was overlooked. Every dance routine, every stage setup, and every logistical aspect was double-checked under her watchful eye.

Satisfied with the preparations, Maria gathered her notes and headed to the next meeting. The core group meeting with the school administrators and parent representatives was already in progress. As the appointed teacher representative, Maria was a vital link between the faculty and the broader school community.

"Welcome, Maria," greeted Ms. Santos, the new principal, as Maria took her seat. "We were just discussing the funding for our upcoming school projects."

Maria smiled and joined the discussion, sharing updates and insights. They talked about potential sponsors, community partnerships, and creative fundraising ideas. The room buzzed with a collaborative spirit as they brainstormed ways to enhance the students' learning experience and support the school's growth.

After the meeting, Maria couldn't help but feel a profound sense of fulfillment. She was thriving in her roles, balancing the demands of coordinating major school events and representing her colleagues. It was a stark contrast to her life in Lae, and the sense of purpose and community she had missed so dearly was now back, stronger than ever.

As she walked through the bustling hallways of St. Michael's, Maria felt a deep sense of belonging. She was back to the life she had always loved, surrounded by familiar faces and the joyful chaos of school life. Her days were filled with meetings, lesson plans, and the vibrant chatter of students, leaving little room for the past.

She had moved on from Franz, not just physically but emotionally. The memories of Lae were now just a distant chapter in her life story. The pain and confusion had faded, replaced by the excitement and fulfillment of her work. Maria's heart swelled with gratitude for the second chance she had been given to reclaim her happiness and purpose.

In the quiet moments between her busy schedule, she would often reflect on how far she had come. She was no longer the woman struggling to find her place in a foreign land, burdened by unresolved emotions and a turbulent relationship. Instead, she was a respected educator, a beloved colleague, and a pillar of her community.

With Gratitude Day fast approaching, Maria poured her heart into the preparations, eager to create an event that would resonate with the entire school. This celebration was more than just a day of performances and festivities—it was a testament to the strength and unity of St. Michael's, and a personal triumph for Maria as she embraced the life she was always meant to lead.

As Maria embraced her new role and the vibrant life at St. Michael's, she found peace in knowing that her journey had led her exactly where she needed to be. While her plans to work overseas hadn't materialized as she had hoped, she trusted in God's plan and believed that her time would come. It might not be abroad, but she was confident that she was fulfilling her purpose right where she stood.

Chapter 31: A Familiar Melody

The aroma of freshly brewed coffee mingled with the comforting scent of Lola's signature banana bread, a fragrance that always brought a wave of nostalgia washing over Maria. Sunlight streamed through the expansive windows of their childhood home, illuminating the faces gathered around the well-worn dining table. Today was a day of celebration—Miguel, her dependable younger brother, had finally received the promotion he'd been working towards with unwavering dedication.

Maria loved moments like this. The warmth of family enveloped her, a stark contrast to the cold loneliness that had seeped into her life lately. Here, amidst the shared laughter and heartfelt conversations, a sense of belonging rekindled within her. Memories flickered to life—their parents' voices, a constant reminder that education was the key to a better future, echoing through the years.

"Miguel!" Maria exclaimed, her voice brimming with pride as she reached across the table to squeeze his hand. "Senior analyst! That sounds incredible! We're all so incredibly proud of you."

Miguel chuckled, a hint of relief mixed with the pride etched on his face. "It's been a long road. But seeing the look on all your faces makes it all worth it. Thanks for always believing in me, even when I doubted myself."

Their parents, seated at the head of the table, beamed with a mixture of pride and fondness. Maria glanced around, taking in the familiar scene—her parents, their faces etched with the lines of a life well-lived, their eyes sparkling with love, and Miguel, now a man in his own right, radiating quiet confidence. It was moments like these, simple and unpretentious—shared meals, church visits, casual hangouts—that filled Maria's heart with a warmth that surpassed any material possession.

"And speaking of accomplishments," Maria added, her gaze shifting towards Lucy, her younger sister, who sat engrossed in a stack of textbooks on the far end of the table. "We can't forget about our scholar here! Graduating top of your class, another Dean's Lister? That's amazing, Lucy."

A blush crept up Lucy's neck, a shy smile gracing her lips. "Thanks, *Ate*. It wouldn't be possible without you guys always supporting me."

The following morning dawned bright and crisp, the perfect start to a familiar Sunday routine. After a breakfast filled with laughter and warm conversation, Maria and her family made their way to church together, a tradition they'd cherished since childhood.

The bustling food court transported Maria back to their childhood in Manila, where their parents would treat them to Jollibee after Sunday service. As they shared stories and enjoyed their meals, a different kind of warmth bloomed within her. This wasn't just about reliving the past; it was about building a bridge to the future, a future where the joy of family remained the strongest foundation, a future where education, the value her parents instilled in them all, would pave the way for a brighter tomorrow.

Chapter 32: Tinder Surprise

Sunlight filtered through the gaps in the curtains, painting dancing streaks across Maria's eyelids. A delicious aroma, like warm vanilla and fresh fruit, tickled her nose, coaxing her awake. A smile tugged at her lips. Birthdays. Even at 30, her family still held onto their traditions.

A chorus of perfectly harmonized singing shattered the peaceful morning. "*Happy Birthday to you...*" The door creaked open, revealing her family, all smiles and mismatched sleepwear, crowding the doorway. Miguel, ever the jokester, held a lopsided cake adorned with thirty flickering candles.

"Thirty candles, huh?" Maria chuckled, accepting the cake with a feigned grimace. "Trying to set off the fire alarm, Miguel?"

"Hey, it wouldn't be a birthday without a little excitement," he winked, earning a playful swat on the arm from their mother.

The morning unfolded in a familiar rhythm—laughter, shared stories, and the inevitable teasing about Maria's single status.

"Thirty years old, Maria," her mother chided gently, a playful glint in her eyes, "and still no husband on the horizon? You know your father and I were once the hottest singing duo in

Pampanga! We'd love some grandchildren to carry on the musical legacy, wouldn't we, Papa?"

Her father, a man whose voice could still melt hearts, chuckled. "We wouldn't want you to be the only songbird in the family, would we, *anak*?"

Maria felt a familiar pang of guilt. A past relationship had left its mark, making her wary of rushing into anything serious. Yet, as she listened to her family's playful banter, a tiny seed of curiosity about exploring new possibilities began to sprout within her.

Later that afternoon, Maria met Chu for their usual after-work coffee ritual. As they sipped their lattes, Chu launched into a familiar topic.

"So, Maria," Chu began, her voice conspiratorial, "have you considered my suggestion? Tinder? It's the 21st century, girl! Everyone's on it these days."

"Hmm, not really my thing," Maria demurred. "Besides, I haven't exactly had stellar luck in the love department."

Chu snorted. "Well, with all that work you bury yourself in, who has time for love? Look, even your parents are getting antsy. You can't blame them, you know? Thirty is a milestone birthday."

Maria sighed. Chu was right. Maybe it was time to step outside her comfort zone. "Alright, alright," she conceded. "You win. But if I end up on a date with a guy whose idea of conversation is grunt noises, I'm blaming you."

Chu grinned triumphantly. "Don't worry, with a little profile tweaking, we'll find you Mr. Right in no time. Now, download the app and let's see what kind of dating material the world has to offer."

That night, with a healthy dose of skepticism and a flicker of curiosity, Maria found herself downloading Tinder. The process felt surreal. Swiping through profiles, a strange mix of amusement and apprehension bubbled within her. Were these really the people looking for love?

Suddenly, a profile caught her eye. The picture wasn't anything showy—a man in a well-tailored suit, standing confidently in front of a grand, old building. The architecture looked vaguely European, the kind she'd seen in travel documentaries. The man himself was an enigma. His features were a captivating blend of ethnicities, defying easy classification. He had a warm smile that crinkled the corners of his eyes, and the caption below the picture read: "Looking for an adventure buddy who appreciates good coffee and even better sunsets." A smile bloomed on Maria's face. Maybe, just maybe, Tinder wasn't such a bad idea after all. With a tentative swipe right, she swiped right, a tiny seed of hope blossoming in her heart.

Chapter 33: A Spark Across the Miles

The air crackled with a joyful energy as the last notes of the closing performance faded. Maria, her smile wide enough to rival the setting sun, basked in the wave of congratulations. The Gratitude Day celebration, a vibrant showcase of Asian cultures spearheaded by her team, had been a resounding success.

"Excellent work, Maria!" boomed Ms. Santos, her booming voice punctuated by a hearty pat on her back. "The energy, the colors, the sheer diversity—it was truly a feast for the senses!"

Teachers and parents alike echoed her sentiment, showering Maria and her team with praise. Watching the students, their faces flushed with excitement as they performed dances from various Asian countries, a pang of wanderlust struck Maria. Each performance was a window into a different world, a world rich in tradition and vibrant with life.

The captivating rhythm of the Punjabi dance performance lingered in her mind. The colorful costumes, the energetic steps, the infectious joy—it all seemed so alive, so real. A smile bloomed on her face as she recalled how much she'd always loved Bollywood movies, especially the ones from Punjab. They were a source of constant entertainment, filled with music, dance, and larger-than-life stories.

Suddenly, a flicker of inspiration ignited within her. India. That was where the next chapter of her adventures would begin! This wasn't just a fleeting thought; it felt like a spark, a calling to explore a land that had always held a certain mystique for her.

Just then, Chu, her ever-observant friend, sidled up beside her.

"Congratulations, superstar!" Chu exclaimed, wrapping Maria in a tight hug. "You practically brought the entire continent of Asia to life here today!"

Maria chuckled, the warmth of Chu's friendship a familiar comfort. "Thanks, Chu. It wouldn't have been possible without everyone's hard work."

"Speaking of hard work," Chu's voice dropped to a conspiratorial whisper, "have you made any progress on Tinder?"

Maria blushed. "I, uh, actually swiped right on a few profiles. But there's one that really caught my eye."

Intrigue flickered in Chu's eyes. "Spill! What's this mysterious Mr. Right?"

Maria pulled out her phone, a playful smile on her lips. "Well," she began, "he seems a bit mysterious. The picture is outside a beautiful European building, and the caption talks about adventure buddies and sunsets. But the most interesting part? His name is just Mr. R."

Chu burst out laughing. "Mr. R? Maybe it's Mr. Right in disguise!"

Despite the teasing, Maria couldn't help but grin. "We'll see if Mr. R swipes right too," she replied, the playful banter masking a flicker of nervousness.

As if on cue, a notification buzzed on her phone. Maria's heart skipped a beat as she saw the familiar Tinder logo. With trembling fingers, she opened the message. It wasn't just any message—it was from the very profile she'd been discussing with Chu.

The message was simple, yet it sent a thrill through her: "Hi, how are you? I am Raj, from Mumbai, India."

Maria stared at the message, a smile stretching across her face. Was it destiny? A cosmic coincidence? Or perhaps the universe, in its own mysterious way, had just nudged her a little closer to her dream.

Chapter 34: A Mumbai Adventure Beckons

The glow of Maria's phone screen illuminated her face as she exchanged messages with Raj. Their conversations were becoming a welcome daily ritual, filled with lively banter and a genuine curiosity about each other's worlds. She'd confessed her dream of visiting India, and Raj had enthusiastically thrown open the virtual doors to his city. He'd even volunteered to be her guide, offering to send a formal invitation—a gesture that both amused and touched Maria.

Getting to know Raj online provided a clearer picture of the man behind the intriguing profile. His Facebook photos revealed a guy with a warm smile and an easygoing personality. Though raised in India, he'd mentioned having some British ancestry. Family seemed to be a cornerstone of his life—he spoke fondly of caring for his mother and having a brother living abroad. It was a positive detail, but Maria, ever mindful of past experiences, kept a cautious approach. This time, she wouldn't let her heart lead the way.

"So, Maria," Raj's message popped up, brimming with excitement, "Mumbai awaits! Imagine yourself standing at the Gateway of India, the cool sea breeze carrying whispers of history. Or picture the opulent Taj Mahal Palace hotel, a luxurious haven in the heart of the city."

Maria's heart skipped a beat. The iconic landmarks, the vibrant descriptions—it all felt so real. Her fingers flew across the keyboard.

"Those sound amazing, Raj! Is there anything else a first-time visitor like me shouldn't miss?"

Raj's reply came quickly, filled with suggestions. "Mumbai is a feast for the senses, Maria. We could wander through the bustling bazaars of Colaba Causeway, where you can find everything from spices to souvenirs. Or perhaps a boat trip to the Elephanta Caves, a UNESCO World Heritage Site carved with ancient sculptures, would interest you?"

Maria's imagination soared. Exotic markets, ancient caves—the possibilities were endless. She typed back, a hint of wonder in her message.

"Wow, you really know how to paint a picture, Raj! Everything sounds so exciting. Tell me more about the food—any recommendations for a beginner like me?"

The conversation continued, Raj transforming into a virtual travel guide for Maria. He described the city's vibrant culture, its delicious street food scene, and even hinted at hidden gems beyond the tourist trail. Despite the exciting possibilities Mumbai offered, Maria held her emotions in check. This newfound online connection was a chance to explore a new culture, not a fast track to a relationship. With a cautious optimism, she committed to enjoying the journey, one virtual conversation and travel tip at a time.

Chapter 35: Welcome to India

The whirring of the airplane engines faded as Maria touched down at Chhatrapati Shivaji Maharaj International Airport, her heart pounding with anticipation. India, a land of vibrant colors, rich history, and mouthwatering cuisine, awaited her exploration.

This trip held a special significance. Maria had confided in her family about meeting Raj online, emphasizing their current status as just friends getting to know each other. After several video chats, they were all impressed by Raj's sincerity and warmth. This time, they trusted Maria's cautious optimism.

Stepping out of the arrivals gate, a wave of humid Mumbai air washed over her, carrying the symphony of honking horns and a cacophony of street vendors. The sheer vibrancy of the scene was both exhilarating and slightly overwhelming. Maria scanned the sea of faces for a familiar one, a nervous flutter in her stomach.

Suddenly, a broad smile and a wave caught her eye. There stood Raj, even more handsome in person than his pictures. He held a vibrant bouquet of lilies, their fragrant scent a delightful welcome.

"Maria!" he called out, his voice warm and welcoming. "You made it!"

Maria, her face breaking into a wide grin, hurried towards him. "Raj! It's so good to finally meet you in person."

"The feeling is mutual," he replied, handing her the flowers. "Welcome to Mumbai!"

After a warm exchange of greetings, a wave of uncertainty washed over Maria. "So," she started, fiddling with the flowers, "how do you navigate all this?" she gestured vaguely towards the bustling scene around them.

Raj chuckled, his easy smile calming her nerves. "It can be a bit overwhelming at first," he admitted. "But don't worry, I'm your Mumbai guru tonight. Let's grab a taxi."

As they navigated the bustling streets, Maria's eyes darted everywhere, soaking in the vibrant scene. "Wow, the saris are even more stunning in person," she remarked, pointing at a group of women draped in colorful silks. "So many different patterns!"

Raj chuckled, his pleasure evident. "You've done your research, I see! Mumbai is a fashion capital in its own right, with a unique blend of traditional and modern styles."

"It's amazing!" Maria exclaimed, snapping a picture on her phone. "Everything feels so different here."

"Welcome to the magic of India," Raj replied with a wink.

The restaurant, Leopold Cafe, was a delightful surprise. The warm ambiance, the aroma of spices, and the soft strains of Indian music were an assault on the senses in the best way possible. The menu, filled with unfamiliar names, left Maria feeling slightly lost.

"Don't worry," Raj said, amusement dancing in his eyes, "I'll be your guide."

He recommended a *chicken biryani*, a fragrant rice dish with tender chicken and aromatic spices. "It's one of our most popular dishes," he explained. "For the vegetarian option, we have *palak paneer*, a creamy spinach dish with cheese. Both are perfect for someone wanting to try Indian food for the first time."

As Maria took her first bite of the *biryani*, a symphony of flavors exploded in her mouth—warm spices, tender chicken, and fluffy rice. It was unlike anything she'd ever tasted before.

"Wow," she breathed, her eyes wide with delight. "This is incredible! I can't believe I've waited this long to try Indian food!"

Raj chuckled. "There's a whole world of flavors waiting for you, Maria. We'll have to explore some street food stalls tomorrow, shall we?"

The evening unfolded in a flurry of conversation and delicious food. Raj regaled her with stories of his childhood in Mumbai, his passion for his city evident in every word. As he dropped her off at the hotel, he turned to her with a smile. "Welcome to Mumbai, Maria. I have a feeling this is just the beginning of your Indian adventure."

Maria stepped out of the car, a newfound excitement bubbling within her. This trip to Mumbai, with its vibrant sights, delicious food, and the genuine hospitality of Raj, promised to be an unforgettable experience.

Chapter 36: A Deluge of Delights

Sunlight painted the Mumbai sky a vibrant orange as Raj arrived at Maria's hotel, eager to continue their exploration of the city. Maria, equally excited, joined him after a quick breakfast.

They decided to venture beyond the tourist trail, starting their day with a walk along Marine Drive, the scenic coastal road that offered breathtaking views of the Arabian Sea. The salty breeze whipped through their hair as they strolled along the promenade, watching surfers carve through the waves and families enjoying a morning picnic.

"It's even more stunning than in the videos," Maria admitted, inhaling the fresh air. "I can see why they call it the Queen's Necklace."

Raj grinned. "Just wait till you see Bandra later. It's a vibrant neighborhood known for its street art and trendy cafes."

True to his word, Bandra was a kaleidoscope of color and energy. Murals splashed across buildings, depicting everything from Bollywood stars to social commentary. Cozy cafes with outdoor seating offered a chance to people-watch and soak up the atmosphere.

Hunger pangs started to gnaw at their bellies, leading them to a bustling street food stall. Raj, ever the guide, helped Maria navigate the unfamiliar menu.

"You have to try the *pani puri*," he suggested, pointing to a picture. "Crispy, hollow puris filled with a delicious potato mixture and tangy water—a real explosion of flavors in your mouth!"

Maria took a tentative bite, her eyes widening in delight. The textures and flavors were unlike anything she'd ever experienced. The crispy shell yielded to a burst of tangy water and spiced potato filling, creating a delightful symphony in her mouth.

"Wow, this is incredible!" she exclaimed, dabbing her forehead with a napkin. "The street food here is amazing!"

Raj chuckled. "There's more where that came from. How about we try some sweets next?"

He led her to a nearby sweet shop, where the display cases overflowed with colorful treats. Maria pointed to a glistening ball of dough, nestled in a pool of sugar syrup.

"What's that?" she asked curiously.

"That's a *gulab jamun*," Raj explained. "A deep-fried dough ball soaked in a sweet, rose-flavored syrup. It's practically a national dessert!"

Maria took a bite, the warm, syrupy sweetness filling her mouth. It was a decadent treat, a perfect ending to their spicy adventure.

As the day wore on, they explored more of Mumbai's hidden gems, sharing stories and laughter along the way. By evening, Raj extended a warm invitation.

"Maria," he began, a hint of nervousness in his voice, "I'd love for you to meet my mother, Esha, in person. You've already spoken to her on video calls, but I'd love for you to experience her hospitality firsthand."

Maria felt a warmth spread through her chest. Meeting Esha in person felt like a natural progression of their online connection, and a chance to experience a home-cooked Indian meal.

Raj's home was a warm and welcoming space. The entrance was adorned with beautiful marigold garlands, a sign of auspiciousness. Inside, the aroma of spices filled the air, emanating from the kitchen. Esha, her face etched with kindness and wisdom, greeted them with a warm smile.

"Maria!" she said, her voice soft and melodic. "We've already met virtually, but it's so wonderful to see you in person! Welcome, *beta*."

Maria, touched by Esha's warmth, returned the greeting respectfully. Esha, as Maria had already seen in the video calls, turned out to be a deeply religious woman. A small altar adorned with fresh marigolds held pictures of Hindu deities—Lord Shiva with his wife Parvati, Lord Ganesha, and even a framed picture of Sai Baba.

As they settled in, Esha regaled them with stories of Raj's childhood, her eyes twinkling with pride. "He was always such a good boy," she said, looking fondly at her son. "Always helping others, putting his family first."

Maria couldn't help but steal a glance at Raj, who sat beside her, a faint blush creeping up his neck. Esha presented a delicious spread for dinner—crispy, golden *aloo parathas*, stuffed with spiced potatoes and served with a side of tangy pickles and cool, creamy *raita*. The meal was a revelation for Maria, showcasing the depth and complexity of Indian cuisine beyond her favorite, *chicken biryani*.

The evening flowed with conversation, laughter, and a heartwarming sense of connection. As Raj walked Maria back to her hotel, a comfortable silence settled between them. The stars twinkled above, mirroring the warmth in Maria's heart.

"Thank you for inviting me to your home, Raj," Maria said sincerely. "It was wonderful meeting your mother."

The pleasure was all ours, Maria," Raj replied, his voice a low murmur. "I had a wonderful time today. Maybe tomorrow, we can explore some historical sites? The Gateway of India and the Taj Mahal Palace Hotel are architectural marvels you wouldn't want to miss."

A pleasant warmth spread through Maria's chest. The day had been filled with delicious food, vibrant sights, and heartwarming conversations. Meeting Esha had been a highlight, and seeing Raj interact with his mother had given her a glimpse into his softer side.

"That sounds fascinating," Maria agreed, a smile playing on her lips. "And tomorrow, how about we try some Punjabi cuisine for lunch? I'm eager to experience the full spectrum of Indian flavors."

Raj's eyes lit up. "Punjabi food, absolutely! There's this fantastic little place near the Gateway that does the most incredible *sarson ka saag*—a mustard greens curry that'll knock your socks off. We can pair it with some fluffy *makki di roti*—a perfect Punjabi combination."

They continued chatting excitedly about their plans for the next day, a comfortable silence settling between them every now and then. As Raj walked Maria back to her hotel, the city lights twinkled around them like scattered diamonds.

"Thank you for a wonderful day, Raj," Maria said sincerely, stopping at the entrance. "I can't wait to see what tomorrow brings."

Raj's smile was warm and genuine. "Me neither, Maria. Until tomorrow then."

With a final wave goodbye, Maria entered the hotel, her heart brimming with a newfound sense of connection. This trip to Mumbai was blossoming into something more than just a cultural exploration. It was strengthening their friendship, forging a bond built on shared experiences and a growing appreciation for each other's cultures.

Chapter 37: A Tapestry of Faith and Friendship

The sun cast a warm glow on Mumbai as Raj and Maria hailed a taxi. "Ready to some iconic landmarks for day two?" Raj asked with a grin.

"Absolutely!" Maria replied, her eyes sparkling with anticipation.

Their first stop was the majestic Gateway of India, a grand archway built in the early 20th century to commemorate the visit of King George V and Queen Mary. As they approached the monument, its intricate stonework and imposing presence left Maria speechless.

"Wow," she breathed, taking in the details. "It's even more impressive in person than in the pictures."

Next, they made their way to the iconic Taj Mahal Palace Hotel. The imposing structure, with its elegant dome and colonial architecture, exuded an atmosphere of luxury and grandeur. They wandered through the opulent lobby, marveling at the high ceilings, crystal chandeliers, and historic photographs.

"It's like stepping back in time," Maria remarked, her voice hushed with awe.

"Indeed," Raj replied. "The Taj has been a symbol of Mumbai's heritage for over a century."

As they exited the hotel, the golden light of the setting sun painted the sky in hues of orange and pink. They hailed a taxi and soon found themselves seated in a cozy restaurant, the air fragrant with exotic spices. As they savored the rich flavors of the Punjabi dishes, Maria couldn't help but agree with Raj's earlier statement. This truly was a taste of history.

"Thank you for showing me around today, Raj," she said sincerely. "I've truly fallen in love with Mumbai."

Raj smiled warmly. "It's my pleasure, Maria. I'm glad you're enjoying your time here."

The next day, Raj surprised Maria with a trip to Lonavala, a hill station nestled in the Western Ghats, offering a refreshing escape from the bustling city. The scenic drive unfolded before them, revealing lush greenery, cascading waterfalls, and breathtaking views of the valley below.

"This place is beautiful!" Maria exclaimed, taking in the fresh mountain air.

"Lonavala is a perfect getaway for Mumbai residents," Raj explained. "We can go for a hike later, or just relax and enjoy the scenery."

They spent the day exploring the hill station, visiting the famous wax museum, enjoying a boat ride on the serene lake, and indulging in delicious local street food. As the sun began to set, they arrived at Tiger's Leap, a dramatic cliff overlooking a deep valley.

Standing at the edge, Maria felt a sense of awe and a tinge of vertigo. "This view is incredible," she said, her voice barely a whisper.

Raj placed a reassuring hand on her shoulder. "Careful there," he chuckled. "Don't worry, I've got you."

Maria couldn't help but admire Raj's constant attentiveness and care throughout the trip. He had never once crossed a line or made her feel uncomfortable, a quality she deeply appreciated.

Later that evening, while strolling through the town, they stumbled upon a beautiful Catholic church. The sound of hymns emanating from within piqued Raj's curiosity.

"Would you mind if we go in for a bit?" Raj asked, a hint of hesitation in his voice.

Maria, surprised by his request, tilted her head. "Of course not. I would love to see it and pray." she replied, curious about his reason.

Inside, the church was bathed in the warm glow of candlelight, creating a peaceful and serene atmosphere. As they sat quietly in a pew, Raj closed his eyes and bowed his head in prayer. Maria watched him, touched by his quiet devotion despite his Hindu upbringing.

"My grandmother used to take me to church when I was little," Raj explained afterwards, a hint of nostalgia in his voice. "She believed in the importance of respecting all faiths."

Maria found his openness refreshing. This trip to India wasn't just about exploring a new culture; it was about discovering a new depth to the man she was getting to know.

The following day, with a heavy heart, Maria decided to embark on a solo trip to Agra to see the Taj Mahal, a lifelong dream. While a part of her longed to explore Punjab with Raj, she knew her limited time wouldn't allow it. However, as she boarded the train, a promise bloomed within her. This wouldn't be her last visit to India, and she couldn't wait to return and explore more with Raj by her side.

Chapter 38: Reflections and Resolutions

Maria was immersed in the flurry of graduation preparations, her desk buried under piles of ceremony programs, diploma covers, and a checklist that seemed endless. The air buzzed with the excitement of impending celebration, and Maria's mind was equally full. She barely noticed Chu entering her office until she heard her friend's familiar voice.

"Maria, you're a whirlwind of activity," Chu remarked, leaning against the doorframe with an amused smile.

Maria paused, looking up with a warm smile. "It feels like it. But I'm just trying to make sure everything goes perfectly for the kids. This is their big moment."

Chu's eyes sparkled with excitement. "I can't believe you've managed all this while also planning your trip to India. How's everything coming together?"

Maria's face brightened at the mention of her upcoming journey. "It's all set. My family is thrilled for me. They know how much this trip means. And honestly, I can't wait to go back. Meeting Raj and his family was such an eye-opener. They were incredibly kind."

Chu raised an eyebrow, her curiosity evident. "You've mentioned Raj quite a bit. Is he that special to you now?"

Maria chuckled, a blush creeping into her cheeks. "He's just... different. I admire him and his family a lot. They've shown me such kindness. But I'm being careful. I've learned from the past, and I want to make sure I'm looking for a partner, not just a fleeting romance."

Chu nodded, understanding. "That's wise. It's important to know what you want and take your time."

Maria sighed, a thoughtful look crossing her face. "Exactly. I'm thinking about the future. I want something real and lasting."

Their conversation was cut short by the sound of the school bell. It was time for the graduation practice. Maria gathered her things and headed to the auditorium, where the students were already assembling for their rehearsal.

The large room buzzed with anticipation. Senior high school students, dressed neatly in their uniforms, stood in groups, chattering excitedly. This year's graduation was particularly special because it was the first time the school would be graduating a batch of Grade 12 students under the new K-12 curriculum.

Maria moved through the crowd, offering gentle reminders and encouragement. "Remember to smile when you walk across the stage. And keep your steps in time with the music," she advised a group practicing their procession.

Ms. Santos, the principal, approached Maria, her eyes reflecting pride. "You've done an incredible job, Maria. This ceremony is going to be unforgettable."

Maria beamed at the compliment. "Thank you, Ms. Santos. It's been a lot of work, but seeing how excited the students are makes it all worthwhile. They deserve a perfect day."

Ms. Santos nodded, looking out at the bustling scene. "They'll remember this forever, thanks to your dedication."

As the final practice session drew to a close, Maria stood back and watched the students perform their graduation song. The melody filled the auditorium, their voices blending in harmony. Tears welled up in Maria's eyes as she absorbed the moment, filled with pride and nostalgia.

The day of the graduation ceremony arrived swiftly. The auditorium was packed with proud parents, teachers, and friends, all eager to celebrate this milestone. Maria's heart swelled with emotion as she watched the students process in, their faces glowing with pride and anticipation.

The ceremony unfolded flawlessly. Speeches were heartfelt, diplomas were awarded with cheers, and the graduation song resonated through the hall, a bittersweet farewell to their school days and a hopeful welcome to their future. Maria clapped and cheered, tears streaming down her cheeks as she watched the culmination of their hard work and dedication.

As the event concluded and the graduates and guests began to leave, Maria lingered near the stage, soaking in the aftermath of the celebration. Suddenly, a familiar voice called out to her.

"Maria? Is that really you?"

Turning, Maria saw Christine, an unexpected face from her past. Christine approached, her eyes wide with recognition and warmth.

"Christine," Maria said, a mix of surprise and delight in her voice. "How are you?"

Christine offered a tentative smile, her expression a mixture of hope and hesitation. "I'm doing well, Maria. It's been so long. How have you been?"

Maria blinked back the day's emotions, her voice steady but soft. "I've been good. Busy, but good. It's really nice to see you again."

Christine's gaze softened. "I've been thinking about you a lot. I wanted to say I'm sorry about what happened in Papua New Guinea with Dean. I didn't know what to do to help you at that time."

Maria shook her head, offering a gentle smile. "Let's not dwell on the past, Christine. We've both moved on. It's okay."

Christine nodded, relief washing over her face. "Thank you, Maria. I'm back in the Philippines now, looking for a teaching job. I've missed it so much. Teaching was always such a big part of my life, like it is for you."

Maria's eyes lit up. "That's wonderful news, Christine. It's great that you're getting back into something you love. We should catch up properly sometime."

As they chatted, the memories of their shared past mingled with the excitement of their reunion. It was a poignant reminder of how far Maria had come and the new chapters still to be written.

Later that evening, as Maria lay in bed, she reflected on the day's events and her conversation with Christine. Throughout her journey, her faith had been her anchor, guiding her through the highs and lows. She whispered a heartfelt prayer, filled with gratitude and hope for the future.

Chapter 39: Crossroads of Dreams

Maria and Christine sat at a cozy café, the aroma of freshly brewed coffee mingling with the soft hum of conversations around them. Since their unexpected reunion, the two had rekindled their old friendship, catching up on lost time and sharing the turns their lives had taken. Today, Christine had exciting news that she couldn't wait to share.

Christine leaned in, her eyes alight with enthusiasm. "Maria, I've got something incredible to tell you. I've been offered a teaching job in the US through a cultural exchange program. It's a five-year stint, and I'll be there on a J-1 visa."

Maria's eyes widened in surprise. "Wow, Christine, that's amazing! How did you find out about it?"

Christine grinned, her excitement palpable. "A friend mentioned it to me. They're looking for teachers from different countries to bring new perspectives to their schools. It's such a fantastic opportunity to teach and travel."

Maria listened intently, her mind swirling with thoughts. "It sounds like a dream come true. What's the process like? Is it difficult to get in?"

Christine shook her head. "Not at all. The application is straightforward, and the best part is that there's no placement fee. You only have to pay for your documents and visa application. With your experience and passion, I think you'd be a perfect fit."

Maria's thoughts began to race. The idea of teaching in the US, a country she had long dreamt of visiting, stirred a mix of excitement and apprehension within her. It wasn't just the allure of a new job; it was a chance to rewrite her story, to live out her dreams of traveling the world while doing what she loved.

"Do you really think I should apply?" Maria asked, her voice tinged with uncertainty.

Christine reached across the table, touching Maria's hand reassuringly. "Absolutely. You've always wanted to explore and see the world, and this is your chance. Plus, you'll get to experience teaching in a completely different environment. It's a win-win."

Maria nodded slowly, her mind drifting to her childhood dreams. She remembered watching her relatives jet off to America with a mixture of envy and longing, wishing she had the means to explore far-off places. "I've always wanted to see the US It's been a dream of mine for as long as I can remember. I used to promise myself that one day, I'd find a way to get there."

Christine smiled warmly. "Then maybe this is the sign you've been waiting for. It's an opportunity to fulfill that promise to yourself. Think of all the possibilities it could open up for you."

The thought of leaving St. Michael's, her beloved students, and her family weighed heavily on Maria's heart. She had found a deep sense of purpose and belonging in her role at the school. But the call of adventure and the chance to explore a new world was equally compelling.

"It's just... I've finally settled here. I love teaching at St. Michael's, and the students mean so much to me. But the idea of living in the US, experiencing new things—it's tempting," Maria confessed, her voice tinged with emotion.

Christine nodded understandingly. "I know it's a tough decision. But you've got to do what feels right for you."

As they continued their conversation, the enormity of the decision loomed over Maria. That evening, she knelt by her bedside, whispering a heartfelt prayer for guidance and clarity.

As she lay in bed, Maria reflected on Christine's words and the promise she had made to herself so long ago. Perhaps this was indeed her second chance, a divine nudge towards a new chapter in her life. It was a crossroads of dreams, where the familiar comfort of home met the exhilarating possibilities of the unknown.

In this chapter of her life, Maria knew she would have to weigh her heart's desires carefully. With God's guidance, she would find the courage to make the choice that would lead her to the life she was meant to live.

Chapter 40: The Road Ahead

Maria sat across from her parents, the warmth of the kitchen enveloping them in a comforting embrace. The familiar clinking of utensils and the scent of her mother's *kare-kare* filled the room. But today, the air was thick with anticipation. Maria had something significant to share.

"Mama, Papa, I've made a decision," Maria began, her voice steady but her heart pounding. "I want to apply for a teaching position in the United States. If I'm accepted, I'll be teaching in a public school in North Carolina."

Maria's parents exchanged worried glances. Her father was the first to speak, his voice gentle but concerned. "North Carolina? That's far from home, Maria. Are you sure this is what you want?"

Maria nodded, her determination evident. "Yes, Papa. It's part of a cultural exchange program for teachers. It's an incredible opportunity for me to grow professionally and personally. I've always dreamed of seeing the world, and this could be my chance."

Her mother's eyes filled with a mixture of pride and worry. "We understand, Maria. We've seen how passionate you are about teaching and your desire to explore. We just want you to be safe and happy."

Maria reached out, squeezing her mother's hand reassuringly. "Thank you, Mama. I know it's a big step, but it's something I've thought about a lot. I promise to stay in touch and visit whenever I can."

Her father nodded slowly, his expression softening. "We'll miss you, Maria. But we want you to spread your wings and chase your dreams. We're proud of you."

A few days later, Maria sat nervously in front of her laptop, preparing for her initial interview with the cultural exchange program. This was a crucial step toward making her dream a reality. The interviewer's friendly demeanor put her at ease as they discussed her experience and passion for teaching.

The conversation shifted to practicalities. The interviewer mentioned, "Maria, you should be aware that public transportation in North Carolina isn't as extensive as you might be used to. To get around, especially in suburban areas, you'll likely need a car. Have you considered this?"

Maria had anticipated this topic. "Yes, I've looked into it. I'm planning to buy a car once I arrive so I can manage my commute to work independently."

The interviewer nodded approvingly. "That's a smart move. Having a car will give you more flexibility. It's good to see you're thinking ahead."

The interview wrapped up on a positive note, leaving Maria hopeful and excited about the future.

Later that evening, Maria's Aunt Luisa joined the family for dinner. She was on holiday, visiting from her long-time home in the Philippines, and had once taught in California under a similar program. She listened intently as Maria shared her plans.

"Maria, teaching in the US is a fantastic opportunity," her aunt began. "But remember, the students there can be quite different from what you're used to in the Philippines. They're often more outspoken and can sometimes be challenging to manage. It's important to be prepared for that."

Maria nodded, absorbing her aunt's advice. "I understand, *Tita*. I've heard that classrooms in the US can be quite different. I'm ready to adapt and learn as much as I can."

Her aunt continued, "Also, about getting a car—I managed without one for a while in California because the public transport was decent. Maybe you should wait until you're sure it's necessary."

Maria respected her aunt's opinion but had also done thorough research. "Thank you, *Tita*. I appreciate your advice. But

North Carolina's public transportation isn't as reliable as California's. I've spoken to other Filipino teachers there, and they've all suggested getting a car. I think it's the best way for me to be independent and not worry about my daily commute."

Her aunt smiled, understanding Maria's determination. "You've clearly thought this through. Just be careful and plan everything well."

Maria felt more resolved than ever. "I will, *Tita*. This is my second chance to explore the world and live out my dreams. I want to do it right."

That night, Maria called Raj to share her plans. His voice was warm and supportive as always.

"Raj, I have some exciting news. I'm applying for a teaching job in North Carolina. If everything goes well, I'll be moving to the US soon," Maria said, her voice brimming with excitement.

Raj's response was immediate and full of encouragement. "Maria, that's incredible! I'm so happy for you. It's a wonderful opportunity. You've always wanted to explore and see the world. This could be your chance."

Maria felt a wave of gratitude wash over her. "Thank you, Raj. Your support means a lot to me. It's a big step, but I feel ready for it."

"Just remember to stay true to yourself and follow your heart," Raj advised. "You have the potential to achieve so much. Don't let anything hold you back."

Maria smiled, feeling a renewed sense of confidence. "I won't. I'm ready to take this step and see where it leads me."

As Maria lay in bed that night, she reflected on the path ahead. The decision to move to the US was daunting, filled with both excitement and uncertainty. But she felt a deep sense of peace knowing that she was following her heart and pursuing her dreams.

Chapter 41: Whispers of Fate

Maria had made a brave decision to resign from her teaching position, dedicating her time to preparing for her new journey, hoping to secure a teaching job in the US She also wanted to spend quality time with her family before the potential move. Despite her best efforts, a month had passed, and she still hadn't received an offer from a school in the States.

Meanwhile, Christine was ready to embark on her new adventure. She was set to leave for Charlotte, North Carolina, where she had secured a teaching position. They met for coffee, sharing updates and offering each other support.

"You'll love Charlotte," Christine said with a beaming smile. "The school is fantastic, and the community seems welcoming. You'll find something soon, Maria. I'm sure of it."

Maria tried to mirror Christine's optimism but couldn't shake her worry. "I hope so. It's almost the start of the school year here, and I still don't have any offers. But I'm so happy for you. You've worked so hard for this."

Christine reached across the table and squeezed Maria's hand. "You've done everything right, Maria. Sometimes, things take a little longer to fall into place. Just keep your faith. It'll happen."

Later, as Maria spoke with Raj, he too, echoed Christine's encouragement.

"Maria, you've come so far," Raj said, his voice warm and reassuring. "You'll find a school. Just give it a little more time."

Though his words brought some comfort, Maria's uncertainty grew. She needed a backup plan. With a bit of hope but facing the reality of her situation, Maria decided to apply for a job at a BPO (Business Process Outsourcing) company. This job would provide her with income and the flexibility to resign quickly if a teaching opportunity in the US came through.

The next day, Maria had her medical examination for the BPO job, part of the pre-employment requirements. As she sat in the waiting room, she received a text from Chu, inviting her to attend the Holy Mass for St. Michael's Institute Day celebration. Maria felt a pang of nostalgia and agreed to go. She missed the familiar faces and the community that had been part of her life for so long.

When Maria arrived at the church, she was greeted with warm smiles and hugs from former colleagues and students. It was a comforting reminder of the community she loved. She even joined the choir, singing the hymns with a heart full of hope and gratitude.

During the Mass, Maria prayed fervently. She asked for guidance and the strength to navigate this uncertain period in her life. She prayed for the opportunity to fulfill her dream of teaching in the US, to explore the world, and to make a difference.

After the Mass, Maria returned home, her spirit lifted by the day's events. As she walked through the door, she saw her mother in deep conversation with their neighbor, Dora, who was known in the community as a *manghuhula*, or fortune teller.

"Maria, come here," Dora called out with a knowing smile. "Let me see your palm."

Maria had always been skeptical of fortune-telling but didn't want to seem rude. She extended her hand. Dora studied Maria's palm intently, her eyes narrowing as if peering into the future.

"I see a lot of money coming your way soon," Dora announced, her voice tinged with mystery. "And I see you purchasing a car within this month."

Maria and her mother exchanged puzzled glances. Though Maria didn't believe in fortune-telling, Dora's words lingered in her mind. The mention of money and a car within the month struck a chord with her deepest hopes. Could it be a sign? She left the conversation feeling a strange mixture of curiosity and disbelief, her thoughts swirling with the possibilities that might be waiting just around the corner.

And as if to punctuate the day's strange twists and turns, her phone buzzed with an unexpected notification that night. It was an interview invitation—from Goldsboro Academy in North Carolina.

Chapter 42: Visa Day

The air crackled with nervous anticipation as Maria sat amidst her family, their faces beaming with pride. Just moments ago, she had shared the news—she had landed the job at Goldsboro Academy! The phone calls to Raj, Christine, and Chu were filled with excited chatter and well wishes. Now, the final hurdle stood before her—the US visa interview.

September 8th, the date etched in her mind for her arrival in the US, had come and gone. A delay in securing an interview appointment meant she wouldn't be making the initial deadline. The new date, September 12th, loomed large on the calendar, a constant reminder of the dream within reach.

Her parents were her pillars of support. Her mother accompanied her to the US embassy, arriving far too early in their eagerness. Maria, dressed in formal attire, clutched the neatly arranged documents in her sweaty palms. The air inside the embassy hummed with a nervous energy. Applicants of all backgrounds sat scattered, some faces etched with anticipation, others clouded with a disheartening sadness. Maria saw the glimmer of joy in some eyes as their visas were approved, and the sting of rejection reflected in others. It was a stark reminder of what was at stake.

The security measures were stringent. A long line snaked its way through the building, each applicant meticulously screened before proceeding. Maria inched forward, her throat tightening with each passing moment. Finally, she was second in line for window number 21.

The applicant before her, a young man with hope brimming in his eyes, leaned back with a relieved smile as his visa was approved. A wave of congratulatory whispers rippled through the nearby crowd. But this fleeting joy was extinguished as the woman in front of Maria received the dreaded news—her visa application denied. The woman's shoulders slumped, her face crumpling in despair. The weight of disappointment settled heavily on Maria's chest.

Now, it was her turn. The consul behind the window exuded an air of quiet seriousness. He began with the formalities, asking for her name and purpose for travel. Maria answered each question clearly and concisely, her heart pounding a frantic rhythm against her ribs.

The interview continued, the consul meticulously reviewing her documents. Then came a question that sent a jolt through her. "How much did you pay the program sponsor who assisted you?"

Maria's brow furrowed in confusion. "Paid? Nothing, sir. I secured the job and applied for the visa on my own. I did not pay any placement fee."

The consul's eyes narrowed. He repeated the question, a hint of suspicion creeping into his voice. Startled, Maria reiterated her answer with unwavering honesty.

A long, tense silence followed. Then, the consul reached into his drawer and pulled out a blue form. Maria's heart sank. It wasn't the stamped passport she had envisioned. Her visa application... *denied.*

Chapter 43: Picking up the Pieces

The weight of disappointment pressed down on Maria like a physical burden. *Denied.* The word echoed in her mind, a cruel echo of all her hopes and aspirations.

Her family gathered around her, their faces etched with concern. Miguel, her brother, wrapped a comforting arm around her shoulders. "*Ate*, don't worry," he said, his voice gruff but gentle. "This isn't the end. We'll figure it out together."

Maria's father, standing quietly by, spoke with a calm, steady voice that always managed to bring her comfort. "Always remember, Maria, even the strongest storms pass. And when the sun shines again, you'll find the strength to bloom anew."

Lucy, her younger sister, squeezed Maria's hand. "You're strong, *Ate*. You can get through this."

Tears welled up in Maria's eyes, spilling over as she embraced them. The outpouring of love from her family was a balm to her wounded spirit.

Later, she contacted the program sponsor that had assisted her with the job application. They listened patiently as she recounted the details of the interview, the consul's suspicion about the non-existent placement fee, and the ultimate denial. While they couldn't explain the specific reason, they assured her the door wasn't completely shut. She could reapply in two weeks, and they'd be happy to offer guidance throughout the process.

That night, seeking solace, Maria knelt before the altar in her room. A small statue of the Blessed Mother, a constant companion since childhood, watched over her. "Why, Mama Mary?" she whispered, tears tracing paths down her cheeks. "I prayed so hard for this opportunity."

The answer didn't come in a celestial voice, but in the quiet strength that welled up within her. She wouldn't let this setback define her.

Just then, her phone buzzed. It was Raj. A pang of guilt washed over her. She hadn't wanted to burden him with her disappointment.

"How did it go?" Raj's voice, warm and concerned, filled the room.

Maria took a deep breath. "It wasn't good, Raj. My visa got denied."

Silence stretched on the line for a moment before Raj spoke again. "Oh, Maria. I'm so sorry."

She could hear the empathy in his voice, and it brought a fresh wave of tears. But then, his tone shifted, firm yet gentle. "Don't give up, Maria. You worked so hard for this dream. Reapply. They can't keep a good teacher down forever."

Maria hesitated. The sting of rejection was still raw, a burning ember in her chest. Tears welled up again, blurring her vision. Raj's encouraging words resonated in her ears, but the fear of putting herself out there only to be denied again felt crippling. Images of the hopeful faces at St. Michael's flashed through her mind, then the excitement of Christine's new life, a stark contrast to her own stalled dream. Doubt gnawed at her. Could she muster the strength to face another possible rejection?

Raj, sensing her internal struggle, spoke again, his voice a soothing balm. "Maria, I know this is hard. Rejection hurts. But remember why you started this journey. Remember the passion that ignited your desire to teach in the States, to explore a new culture, to make a difference. A setback doesn't diminish the validity of those dreams."

A flicker of her old determination flickered in Maria's eyes. Raj was right. This wasn't about proving anything to the consul, it was about fulfilling her own aspirations. The fear of rejection was a formidable foe, but so was the fear of regret, of letting this opportunity slip through her grasp.

Taking a deep breath, Maria felt a newfound resolve settle within her. Wiping away her tears, she met Raj's voice with a determined tone. "You're right, Raj. I won't give up. I'll reapply. This may be a detour, but it won't derail my dream.

Chapter 44: Under the Watchful Gaze of Mary

Hope, like a fragile seedling pushing through cracked pavement, sprouted anew in Maria's heart. The interview on October 7th loomed large on the calendar, a date circled with both anticipation and a flicker of apprehension. But this time, she had a secret weapon—a follow-up interview on September 24th.

One breezy afternoon, a notification while video calling with Raj and his mother, Esha, sent a jolt of excitement through the airwaves. An email from the US embassy announced a follow-up interview. Maria's parents, alerted immediately, erupted in cheers that echoed through the phone. Esha, her warm smile radiating through the screen, exclaimed, "I will pray to Sai Baba for you, Maria. I will write a letter and put it in the altar for your success!"

Raj's eyes sparkled. "This is it, Maria! Look what a star you are! It's time for you to shine in the US."

The 24th arrived, and this time, Maria chose strength over support. The memory of her parents' worried faces after the first denial was still too raw. But she found solace in meeting other Filipino teachers from the same program sponsor, all facing similar follow-up interviews. Sharing their anxieties and hopes fostered a sense of camaraderie.

A knot of dread tightened in her stomach as she saw her previous interviewer, the stern consul from window 17, processing applicants. Relief washed over her when, just before her turn, a staff member approached him and spoke in hushed tones. The consul nodded and gestured towards window 23.

When her turn finally came at window 23, she approached a new consul, a woman with a kind smile. The interview unfolded, and when the inevitable question arose about placement fees, Maria delivered her prepared explanation calmly.

The consul listened intently. Finally, the words Maria had longed to hear filled the air: 'Your visa application has been approved. You can claim your passport after five working days."

Euphoria washed over Maria. Tears welled up in her eyes, blurring her vision. This wasn't just a visa; it was a passport to a new chapter in her life, a testament to her perseverance.

On her way back home, overwhelmed with joy, she called her family and Raj. Stepping back into her house, she was enveloped in a warm embrace by her family. Tears streamed down her cheeks this time, tears of relief and gratitude.

That night, overcome with gratitude, Maria knelt before the altar. A silent prayer of thanks rose from her heart, directed to God for his guidance and unwavering support throughout this challenging journey. As she rose, her eyes fell first upon the statue of St. Michael, the warrior angel. A silent message of thanks passed between them. He had been a source of strength during moments of doubt, his unwavering presence a reminder to fight for her dream.

Next, her gaze landed on the gentle face of the Blessed Mother. A realization dawned on her. All the significant events in this journey—the job offer, the interviews, and now finally, the approval—had all coincided with Marian feasts. A quiet smile touched her lips. It felt like a message, a divine orchestration, a reassuring touch from a higher power.

Reaching for her phone, Maria felt compelled to share her story on Facebook. Her words, filled with hope and resilience, were more than just a personal update; they were a beacon of inspiration for others chasing their own dreams. The journey, she knew, wouldn't be easy, but with faith, determination, and a little bit of divine help, anything was possible.

Chapter 45: Facebook Post 1

FAITH, HOPE AND LOVE.

What do you do when you hit rock bottom? Never stop dreaming, and never doubt the goodness of God. He works wonders in his own time, and his timing is always perfect. THANK YOU, LORD!

The journey wasn't always smooth sailing. During the interview, I explained that the program sponsor facilitating my job application did not charge any such fee, but there seemed to be some confusion on their end. However, divine intervention seemed to play a role when the program sponsor itself intervened and cleared up the confusion with the embassy. This led to my follow-up interview. Honesty truly is the best policy, and I wouldn't change a thing about my answers. The Lord has delivered me—He is good, all the time!

They say a grateful heart attracts miracles, so let me express my deepest gratitude to those who supported me:

To Mama and Papa, you witnessed my struggles and showered me with unwavering love and prayers. Your love is my foundation. To Miguel, Lucy, Chu, and Christine, my prayer warriors—your belief in me never wavered, and I am eternally grateful.

A special thank you to my friend Raj, who constantly pushed me to reach for the stars. Every day, I thank God for bringing you into my life. You and Esha Maa are blessings in disguise. I know you both prayed fervently for this, and Esha Maa, your love transcends blood ties. Waking up at 4 am to pray for me and writing a letter to God on my behalf—your actions touched me deeply. You are the family I found, and together, we move forward!

I couldn't help but sense a deeper meaning in the journey unfolding around significant Marian feasts, a subtle whisper of guidance carried on the wind—

Aug. 5: Dedication of the Basilica of Our Lady of the Snows (job offer received)

Sept. 8: Birthday of Mama Mary (expected arrival in USA, later rescheduled)

Sept. 12: Feast of the Holy Name of Mary (1st consular interview)

Sept. 24: Commemoration of Mary Help of Christians (follow-up interview and visa approval)

Oct. 7: Feast of Our Lady of the Rosary (2nd interview unnecessary due to approval)

These coincidences felt like divine guidance, reminding me that I was on the right path. I trusted, and miracles unfolded right before my eyes.

And to St. Michael, the warrior angel, a silent thank you. Your strength gave me courage during moments of doubt. Your presence reminded me to fight for my dream.

So, when you hit rock bottom, remember:

Keep the FAITH: Trust in a higher power, whatever that may be for you.

Continue to HOPE: Never let go of your dreams.

Spread the LOVE: Surround yourself with supportive people and give back the love you receive.

This is just the beginning. With faith, hope, love, and a touch of divine guidance, I'm ready to embrace this exciting new chapter in North Carolina.

#ToGodBeTheGlory

Chapter 46: A World Away

A bittersweet melody filled the air as Maria hugged her family goodbye at the airport. Tears mingled with smiles as promises of annual reunions were exchanged. With a final wave, she boarded the Japan Airlines flight, her heart a hummingbird trapped in her chest—a mix of excitement and trepidation for the adventure ahead.

The journey unfolded like a travelogue. Narita Airport in Japan, with its gleaming surfaces and robotic efficiency, offered a glimpse into a future filled with technology. Maria chuckled at the self-cleaning toilets, marveling at Japanese innovation while silently vowing to stick to familiar habits.

The smooth Delta Airlines flight carried her onwards, and by the time the plane touched down in Charlotte, the Carolina twilight bathed the city in a warm glow. Exhaustion, tinged with anticipation, washed over her as she stepped off the plane. The elegant facade of The Ivey's Hotel, a Charlotte landmark, greeted her, a beacon of comfort in this new landscape.

Inside the opulent lobby, a friendly staff member with a nametag that read "*Melanie*" approached Maria with a warm smile. "Welcome to The Ivey's, Ms. Rodriguez! Must have been a long journey."

"Yes, that's right," Maria replied, a wave of relief washing over her. "It was a long flight, but I'm excited to be here."

"Excellent! Let me help you with your luggage and get you checked in. Your room is all set, and the other teachers have already arrived." Melanie whisked Maria through the check-in process, her friendly demeanor putting Maria at ease.

Following Melanie, Maria entered a waiting area where a group of educators sat chatting amongst themselves. A mix of nervous excitement hung in the air. Stepping forward, Maria offered a hesitant smile.

"Hi everyone, I'm Maria,' she said, extending her hand.

"Welcome, Maria! I'm Carlos," a Filipino man with a warm grin greeted her, shaking her hand. "This is Ben and Isabel, also from Cebu. And this is Samantha, from Jamaica."

Introductions were exchanged, punctuated by laughter and shared stories of their journeys. Maria found comfort in the familiar Filipino accents and Samantha's infectious enthusiasm. They compared notes on their flights, marveled at the beauty of Charlotte, and shared anxieties about the upcoming orientation.

Later that evening, after a delicious dinner at the hotel restaurant, Maria retreated to her room. The exhaustion of the journey finally caught up with her. But before drifting off to sleep, she pulled out her phone. With a tap of the screen, her family's faces filled the screen, their smiles a balm to her homesickness.

"I finally made it!" Maria exclaimed, her voice thick with emotion.

The sound of excited chatter filled the phone as they bombarded her with questions about her trip and the new city. She shared snippets of her journey, the luxurious hotel, and the friendly teachers she had met. The conversation flowed for what felt like hours, laughter and tears intermingling as they reassured each other of their love and support.

With a heavy heart, she ended the call, promising to update them again soon. Finally, she dialed Raj's number. As his face appeared on the screen, a familiar warmth spread through her.

"Raj! I'm finally in Charlotte!" she announced, a wide smile breaking across her face.

"Maria! Congratulations! How was the flight?" Raj's voice boomed through the speaker, his excitement palpable.

They spent the next hour catching up, sharing details of their days and expressing their elation about Maria's arrival. Raj recounted stories of her mother preparing a special welcome meal for her return, and Maria promised to call them again soon.

With a heart full of gratitude for the day's experiences and a head brimming with new information, Maria drifted off to sleep, ready to embrace the challenges and opportunities that awaited her in North Carolina.

Chapter 47: From Charlotte to Goldsboro

The whirlwind two-and-a-half-day orientation flew by. Yesterday's highlight was a trip to a car dealership, an experience that left Maria buzzing with excitement. She proudly surveyed her new acquisition—a red 2017 Ford Focus with a mere 25,000 miles on the odometer. The dealership even streamlined the process for her, arranging car insurance on the spot. They also explained the legalities of driving with a foreign license. While her Philippine license would be valid for 30 days on North Carolina roads, she had just 14 days to secure her social security number to apply for a North Carolina driver's license. But for now, the key nestled comfortably in her hand, a symbol of newfound independence as she gripped the steering wheel of her very own car.

This afternoon, she would be driving it from Charlotte to Goldsboro, a small town where her teaching position awaited. After a farewell lunch with her fellow teachers, Maria said goodbye, her heart a mix of excitement and apprehension.

A surprise visit from Christine turned their lunch into a joyous reunion. Though it had only been two months since they last saw each other, the anticipation of their meeting added a layer of excitement. Christine, now a seasoned middle school teacher in Charlotte, regaled Maria with stories about her students and the differences between American and Filipino classrooms. Laughter and insightful conversations filled the air as they savored their meal. As the afternoon sun began to cast long shadows, Maria reluctantly said goodbye, her heart brimming with warmth and the soothing voice of Google Maps guiding her on the road ahead.

The drive unfolded like a scene from a road movie—endless stretches of highway, quaint towns blurring by, and the radio playing a mix of unfamiliar tunes. With each passing mile, a sense of accomplishment bloomed within her. She had arrived, navigated a new city, and secured a comfortable haven for herself.

Finally, the exit for Goldsboro loomed ahead. As she turned off the highway, a sense of relief washed over her. Following Christine's instructions, she reached a charming house nestled amidst a quiet neighborhood. A warm smile greeted her as Lita, the Filipina landlady Maria had connected with through a fellow Filipino teacher on the program sponsor's online platform, opened the door. Danny, Lita's American husband, joined them, his handshake firm and friendly.

"Welcome home, Maria!" Lita exclaimed, ushering her inside. "We're so happy to have you here. Come in, come in!"

The apartment, located at the back of their house, was a cozy one-bedroom with a small living room and kitchen. At just $600 a month, it was a steal. Stepping inside, Maria felt a wave of contentment. This would be her home, a haven amidst the unfamiliar, as she embarked on this exciting new chapter in Goldsboro.

"This place is perfect," Maria sighed, dropping her bag on a small couch. "Thank you so much for having me, Ms. Lita."

"Of course, dear," Lita replied, her eyes twinkling. "There's a good number of Filipinos in Goldsboro, you know. You won't feel quite so alone."

Maria's face brightened. "Really? That's wonderful news! Maybe I can find a Filipino grocery store or some restaurants with familiar food."

"Oh, honey, you won't have to look far," Lita chuckled. "There's a whole community here. We even have a Filipino association that holds events sometimes. You'll make new friends in no time, I'm sure."

A wave of relief washed over Maria. The prospect of finding a familiar community in this new town filled her with hope. With Lita's warm welcome and the promise of a Filipino connection, Goldsboro suddenly felt a little less daunting and a whole lot more like home.

Chapter 48: Baptism by Fire

One-day orientation at the district office was a whirlwind, but nothing compared to Maria's first official day at Goldsboro Academy. Excitement bubbled in her chest as she stepped onto the polished school floor. Mr. Carter, the principal, greeted her with a warm smile and a handshake. "Welcome to Goldsboro Academy, Ms. Rodriguez!" his booming voice boomed, shaking her hand firmly. "We're thrilled to have you on board!"

A friendly receptionist named Grace popped out from behind her desk. "Hi Maria! Welcome! I'm Grace, the school receptionist. If you need anything at all, don't hesitate to ask." Her smile was as bright as the sunshine streaming through the window.

Minutes later, Alice, the head of the math department, swept in. Her enthusiasm was infectious as she led Maria on a whirlwind tour of the sprawling school building. "This is the science wing," Alice explained, pointing down a hallway. "And over here, you'll find the library." It seemed to stretch on forever, a vast square of classrooms and hallways. Alice introduced Maria to her fellow math teachers, Tanya and James. Tanya, a woman with warm brown eyes and a gentle smile, offered a reassuring pat on the arm. James, younger with a playful glint in his eyes, joked, "Welcome to the jungle, Ms. Rodriguez! We try to keep things interesting here in the math department."

Finally, it was time to meet her students. Maria learned she would be teaching Foundations of Math to 9th graders for the current semester, with Math 1 following next semester. Adjusting to the American curriculum, she noted the year was divided into semesters, and unlike the Philippines, high school began in 9th grade. Here, public school students enjoyed the freedom of not wearing uniforms.

With a deep breath, Maria entered her 3rd-period class. Nervous energy crackled in the air. As she introduced herself in a clear, confident voice, a sinking feeling settled in her stomach. A tall, lanky boy in the back, sporting a hoodie, snickered. "Yo, did you guys hear that?" he nudged his neighbor, his laughter echoing in the semi-silence. Glancing around the room, she noticed several students doodling in notebooks, their gazes unfocused. A knot formed in her throat.

"Ah," she thought, swallowing past the lump, "this is really going to be a big challenge." But Maria wasn't one to back down easily. Straightening her posture, she met the students' eyes, a determined glint sparkling in her own. "Good morning, class," she said, her voice firm yet friendly. "My name is Ms. Rodriguez, and I'll be your math teacher this semester. Now, who here can tell me what their favorite subject is?"

A beat of silence followed, then a hand hesitantly shot up in the front row. A young girl with bright red glasses beamed at her. "English, Ms. Rodriguez!"

Maria smiled, the tension easing. "Excellent! Maybe you can help me with my English sometime," she joked, earning a ripple of laughter. This small victory fueled her determination. Today might be a baptism by fire, but Maria was ready to prove herself and make a difference in this new classroom.

Later that evening, as exhaustion settled in, Maria craved the familiar comfort of home. With a tap on her phone screen, she connected with her parents. Their faces filled the screen, etched with concern. Eager to downplay the challenges, Maria focused on the positives—Mr. Carter's warm welcome, the helpfulness of her colleagues, and the glimmer of interest in that one student's eyes.

However, when the call ended, a wave of loneliness washed over her. Picking up her phone again, she dialed Raj's number. Hearing his familiar voice filled her with a sense of calm. She poured out the details of her day, the initial discouragement, and the flicker of hope that remained. Raj listened patiently, his voice a steady source of comfort. He shared stories of his own first days at a new school, reminding her of the inevitable learning curve and the importance of perseverance.

As she ended the call, a warmth bloomed in her chest. Raj, her rock, had always been there for her, a constant source of support and encouragement. With renewed determination, Maria knew she could face anything, as long as she had her loved ones, both near and far, cheering her on.

Chapter 49: Kapampangan Kin in Carolina Fields

The crisp Sunday air carried a melody of unfamiliar birdsong as Maria, dressed in her best Sunday attire, ventured out on her own. Lita and Danny had a prior commitment that morning, but they'd assured her they'd connect later. Stepping inside the quaint Filipino church, a wave of warmth washed over her. Gone were the towering steeples and stained-glass windows of her childhood church, replaced by a simpler, more intimate space. Yet, the melodic Tagalog hymns resonated with a familiar comfort, a balm to her soul in this unfamiliar land.

This was Maria's chance to meet some of the Filipinos Lita had introduced her to online. With a mix of excitement and nervousness, she took a seat towards the back, eager to soak in the sights and sounds of a Filipino service abroad. As she scanned the faces around her, a burst of laughter erupted from a pew a few rows ahead. A woman with a smile as vibrant as the tropical flowers adorning the altar turned, her eyes widening in surprise.

"Maria? Is that you?" the woman called out, her voice tinged with a delightful Pampanga accent. Her smile was infectious, and Maria couldn't help but grin back.

"Patrice?" Maria responded, a flicker of recognition lighting up her face. Relief and excitement washed over her as she realized her online connection had come to life. Maria's heart skipped a beat. Finding a fellow Kapampangan in this faraway land felt like a serendipitous gift. "It's so good to see you in person!" Maria exclaimed, relief and excitement warring within her. "How are you?" she added, her voice tinged with a question mark as she gestured for Patrice to join her.

Standing beside Patrice was a gentle-faced woman with soft eyes. "This is Cathy," Patrice introduced her. "Another Kapampangan and a fellow J-1 teacher under the same program sponsor as you, Maria."

Cathy offered a shy smile and a warm handshake. "It's lovely to meet you, Maria. Welcome to Goldsboro."

Across the room, Maria's gaze landed on another familiar face. Regina, another woman she'd connected with online, stood holding hands with a young boy. Recognition dawned on Regina's features, and a smile bloomed on her face. "Maria? What a surprise! How are you doing?"

The unexpected encounter filled Maria with a surge of joy. Patrice, ever the social butterfly, seized the opportunity. "Regina, come join us! This is Maria."

Regina navigated the room with her son, Tommy, in tow, their arrival adding another layer of warmth to the gathering. The conversation flowed effortlessly after the mass, spilling out into the bright Sunday sunshine of the church parking lot, punctuated by bursts of Kapampangan, a language that felt like a secret code shared among friends.

"So, Maria," Patrice began, her voice filled with playful curiosity, "How are you finding life as a teacher in the American South? Still struggling to understand that Southern drawl?"

Maria chuckled. "Honestly, Patrice, it's mostly the students! They're a different breed compared to back home."

Cathy chimed in, her voice a soothing balm. "Don't worry, Maria. We've all been there. Adjusting to a new school system takes time. Besides," she added with a wink, "Patrice here still gets confused by American football!"

The parking lot erupted in laughter, the shared experience fostering a sense of camaraderie. These weren't just colleagues; they were kindred spirits, united by a shared heritage and the unique challenges of navigating a new life in a foreign land.

As lunchtime approached, Patrice announced with a flourish, "I know a fantastic Mexican restaurant downtown—Torreros! My treat. We can continue our catching-up there and enjoy some delicious food that isn't adobo for a change!"

The vibrant atmosphere of the restaurant offered a welcome contrast to the quiet church. Over sizzling fajitas and tangy margaritas, the conversation turned to the joys and challenges of teaching in a new environment. Patrice, a seasoned veteran with several years under her belt, generously dispensed advice and anecdotes.

"Don't be afraid to get creative, Maria," Patrice emphasized, her voice brimming with encouragement. "Adjust your teaching style to suit your students. Remember, it's all about connecting with them and making the learning experience engaging."

Maria soaked in Patrice's words, a newfound sense of confidence blooming within her. As the afternoon sun began its descent, Maria felt a warmth unlike any she'd experienced since leaving home.

Before they parted ways, Patrice extended another invitation. "There's a rosary crusade for Our Lady of Fatima next Saturday at the home of Doctors Alfonso. They're a lovely Filipino couple from Bulacan, and there will be a lot of Filipinos there. You should come, Maria!"

Maria's heart swelled with gratitude. "Thank you so much, Patrice. I wouldn't miss it for the world!"

Later that night, as she video-called her parents, a vibrant energy filled her voice. "Mama, Papa," she exclaimed, "You won't believe it! I met some Filipinos today, all from Pampanga! It feels like I'm starting to build a little piece of home here in Goldsboro," Maria finished, a wide grin stretching across her face. Her parents, their faces illuminated by the screen, beamed back with genuine joy.

"That's wonderful!," her mother interjected, her voice thick with emotion. "It seems God is looking out for you, sending you these kind people to keep you company."

"Absolutely," her father added, a twinkle in his eye. "Tell me more about these new friends of yours. Who is this Patrice you mentioned?"

Maria launched into a detailed account of her day, her voice alight with excitement. She described Patrice's infectious enthusiasm, Cathy's gentle nature, and Regina's sense of humor. She shared the hilarious anecdotes about American football and the comforting familiarity of speaking Kapampangan.

As she spoke, a pang of guilt flickered momentarily. Perhaps she had been painting too rosy a picture of her experience. It wasn't all sunshine and friendly faces. There were still moments of frustration in the classroom, the ever-present longing for her family, and a nagging sense of being an outsider.

But as her parents listened intently, their faces etched with concern and pride, Maria realized something important. Sharing her triumphs, however small, and confiding in them about her struggles, however big, was a way of keeping them close. It was a bridge built across the vast distance, a reminder that their love and support transcended physical boundaries.

"And guess what?" Maria continued, her voice bubbling with anticipation. "Patrice invited me to a rosary crusade next Saturday at the home of a Filipino couple! They say there will be a lot of Filipinos there."

A collective gasp escaped her parents' lips. "Is it safe, *anak*? Are you sure these people are trustworthy?" her mother asked, a hint of worry creeping into her voice.

Maria chuckled, her heart brimming with warmth. "Don't worry, Mama. Patrice seems like a good person, and besides, Regina will be there too. I'll be careful, I promise."

Her parents exchanged a hesitant glance, their concern eventually giving way to a resigned smile. "Okay, *anak*," her father finally conceded. "Just be careful and let us know how it goes."

With a final wave and a promise to call again soon, Maria ended the call. A peaceful silence descended upon the room, broken only by the soft hum of her laptop. A newfound sense of optimism settled within her. Yes, there would be challenges to face, moments of loneliness to endure. But with the support of her family, both near and far, and the growing circle of friends she was building, Maria knew she could navigate anything this new life threw her way

Chapter 50: Beyond Friendship: Whispers of the Heart

The soft glow of her desk lamp cast a warm pool of light on Maria's study table in her living room. Papers from her day at school lay sprawled before her, half-graded word problems competing for attention with a steaming mug of tea. Outside, the street lights were starting to twinkle on, a stark contrast to the peaceful sanctuary she'd created for herself. A gentle chime on her phone startled her from her thoughts. An incoming call. It was Raj.

"Hey, Maria," Raj's voice crackled through the receiver, a familiar warmth washing over her.

"Raj! How's it going?" she forced a cheerful tone, burying the yearning that threatened to spill out.

They chatted about their days, the mundane details tinged with a deeper meaning in the context of their growing connection. Raj described a particularly challenging client, his voice laced with frustration. Maria listened patiently, offering support and advice, her heart ached for him to be closer, to share the burdens and triumphs in person.

The conversation lulled for a moment, a comfortable silence settling between them. Then, Raj spoke, his voice hushed and tentative.

"Maria," he began, "there's something I need to tell you."

Maria's breath hitched. Her mind raced with possibilities, each one sending a jolt of nervous energy through her.

"What is it, Raj?" she managed, her voice barely a whisper.

There was a long pause, the silence stretching between them, thick with unspoken emotions. Finally, Raj spoke again, his voice filled with a quiet intensity.

"This connection we have, Maria," he said, his voice thick with emotion, "it's become more than just friendship for me. The more we talk, the more I get to know you, the deeper my feelings grow. And even though the miles separate us, Maria, I can't deny it anymore. I love you."

Maria's heart pounded in her chest, a hummingbird trapped in a cage of ribs. Her mind was a whirlwind of emotions—surprise, fear, a flicker of something akin to joy. This wasn't what she'd expected, not tonight. Yet, somewhere within her, a truth she couldn't deny anymore bloomed.

"Raj..." she started, her voice trembling slightly. She wanted to deny it, to pretend it wasn't true. Yet, the words wouldn't form.

"Distance can't extinguish what we have, Maria. We can face it together. But," he continued, a new note entering his voice, "there's something else. I applied for a finance consultant position in the UK."

Maria's breath hitched. The UK. Her heart hammered against her ribs, a frantic drumbeat against the sudden vastness of the distance.

"Raj..." the word tumbled out, a mixture of fear and a desperate hope.

"I know," he said, his voice filled with an urgency that mirrored her own. "It's a long shot, but this could be a chance to close the gap. A chance for us."

His words hung in the air, a challenge and a promise. In that moment, staring into the abyss of uncertainty, Maria knew her future, however frightening, was brighter with Raj by her side.

A shaky smile touched her lips. "Alright, Raj," she said, her voice stronger than she felt. "We'll face it together. But for now, promise me you'll fight for that job. And I'll promise you something in return."

A fierce determination replaced the tremor in her voice. "Every night, I'll pray for your success. Because if the universe conspires to bring us together, then I won't let distance stand in our way. And Raj," she added, her voice dropping to a husky whisper, "because... because I love you too."

The line crackled with the weight of their newfound bond, a love story blooming in the face of impossible odds. They ended the call, forever changed, their hearts tethered across the miles by an invisible thread, a promise whispered on a prayer.

Chapter 51: A Phone Too Far

The shrill ring of the bell pierced the hallway, signaling the start of period 2. Maria straightened her shoulders, a confident smile playing on her lips as she entered the classroom. Her 9th-grade math students were already chattering, backpacks strewn across desks and textbooks haphazardly open.

"Alright, class," Maria boomed, her voice cutting through the din. "Settle down and open your textbooks to page 128. Today, we'll be diving into the wonderful world of..." she trailed off, launching into an enthusiastic explanation, equations and diagrams dancing across the whiteboard with a flourish of her marker.

Her eyes, sharp and observant, scanned the classroom, ensuring everyone was engaged. A glint of light from the corner caught her attention. Penelope, was hunched over her phone, completely absorbed in its glowing screen.

Maria's smile softened. "Penelope," she said gently, "can you put your phone away for a moment? We're learning about solving quadratic equations, and your participation is key."

Penelope glanced up, a flicker of defiance replacing her usual attentiveness. "Just a sec," she mumbled, her eyes glued to the phone. "I'm almost done with this."

Maria's voice firmed. "Penelope, focus on the lesson, please. Phones are distracting, not only for you but for others around you."

With a dramatic sigh, Penelope stuffed the phone into her pocket, muttering a complaint under her breath. Maria continued the lesson, but a watchful eye remained on Penelope. A few minutes later, the tell-tale glint of the phone screen reappeared.

Exasperation tinged Maria's sigh. "Penelope," she said, "that's the second time. This is a serious discussion about quadratic formulas, not the latest TikTok trend. Put your phone away and participate in class."

This time, Penelope's defiance exploded. "But," she protested, "it's important! I can't just miss this!"

The classroom fell silent, all eyes fixated on the unfolding scene. Maria took a deep breath, counting to ten in her head to maintain a calm demeanor.

"Penelope," she said evenly, "your phone can wait. This lesson can't. Since you're choosing to disregard the rules, I'm going to have to call Ms. Howard and ask her to send you to ISS."

The threat of In-School Suspension had the desired effect. Penelope's face crumpled. "Ugh, fine," she mumbled, but this time, the phone remained hidden in her pocket. Moments later, a knock on the door announced Mr. Schwarz, the assistant principal, with a stern expression. Penelope gathered her belongings, throwing a defiant glance at Ms. Maria before exiting with Mr. Schwarz in tow.

Silence hung in the air for a beat, then Maria clapped her hands, the sound sharp and purposeful. "Okay, class," she said, her voice back to its usual confident tone, "let's get back on track. Now, where were we with those quadratic equations..."

The class resumed, a newfound quiet settling over the room. It was a small victory, but it served as a reminder: sometimes, it only takes one student to disrupt the flow, but it also only takes one reminder to bring everyone back on course.

The clangor of the dismissal bell cut through the final murmurs of the class. Maria sighed in relief, the tension of the Penelope incident fading with the sound. As she began gathering her things, her phone buzzed in her pocket. A flicker of surprise crossed her face—calls from Paula, her cousin in Florida, were rare occurrences. With a small smile, Maria answered the phone. "Hey Paula, this is a surprise. How are things down in Florida?

"Sunshine and palm trees, Maria! The usual paradise," Paula's voice was bubbly and infectious. "But seriously, how are you doing? I was so excited when you told me you finally made the leap to the States!"

"It's definitely an adjustment," Maria admitted, her voice softer. "Teaching ninth graders keeps me busy, that's for sure."

Paula chuckled. "Still battling teenagers, huh? Don't worry, I remember those days. But hey, listen, I have some amazing news!"

Maria's curiosity piqued. "News? What is it?"

"Well, Thanksgiving break is coming up next month, and after fifteen years down here, I thought it was high time you finally visited Florida!" Paula said, her voice laced with excitement.

"Florida, huh?" Maria said, a hint of wanderlust creeping into her voice. "That's a long way down! But wouldn't it be amazing? Imagine the beaches..."

"Exactly!" Paula interjected. " You know, the kids haven't stopped talking about their Aunt Maria ever since I told them you moved to North Carolina! They're dying to meet you. Think about it, Maria! This would be your first time experiencing Florida sunshine! It would be the perfect chance to relax, catch up, and maybe even trade those fluorescent lights for some beautiful beach sunsets!"

Maria closed her eyes, picturing the white sand and turquoise waters Paula had described. It sounded like a much-needed escape, a world away from the fluorescent lights and controlled chaos of her classroom. The thought of soaking up some sunshine and unwinding on the beach held immense appeal. Perhaps there could even be some time for cultural exploration. After all, Florida wasn't just theme parks (though a quick visit to Disney World or Universal Studios wouldn't be entirely out of the question...). Museums, art galleries, even the chance to explore the Everglades—the possibilities were enticing. This trip could be the perfect blend of relaxation and rejuvenation.

"Alright, Paula," she finally conceded, a newfound excitement in her voice. "You've convinced me. Florida for Thanksgiving sounds amazing. Thank you so much for the invitation!"

"Fantastic!" Paula exclaimed. "You won't regret it, Maria. Now, let me tell you all about the amazing pumpkin pie recipe I'm planning..."

As Maria listened to Paula's enthusiastic chatter, she couldn't help but feel a wave of optimism wash over her. Maybe, just maybe, this trip to Florida would be exactly what she needed to recharge and face the challenges ahead, and it would be even more special reconnecting with relatives in a place called the Sunshine State.

Chapter 52: Sunshine and *Sisig*

Regina pulled the car to a stop at the curb outside Raleigh-Durham International Airport. Maria, a flurry of nervous excitement, gathered her carry-on luggage. The anticipation of seeing her cousin thrummed through her veins.

"So, tell us more about this Raj fellow," Cathy nudged playfully, a knowing smile on her face. Regina had already filled her in on Maria's blossoming long-distance relationship.

Maria blushed. "Well," she began, "we met online a while back, and things just clicked. We talk for hours on the phone, and even though he's miles away, I feel closer to him than anyone I've ever met."

Cathy squeezed Maria's hand. "That's wonderful! Distance can be tough, but true love finds a way, right, Reg?"

Regina, beaming with pride, chimed in, "Absolutely! We're all so happy for you, Maria. You deserve someone who makes you feel that way."

The conversation shifted to lighter topics. "Speaking of feeling good," Regina chuckled, "remember last week's rosary crusade at Dr. Alfonso's house? You wouldn't believe the spread they put out! *Palabok, dinuguan, bibingka...* my mouth is watering just thinking about it."

"Oh, I know, right?" Maria agreed, a nostalgic smile lighting up her face. "And everyone was so welcoming. It was nice to connect with other Filipinos in the area."

The excitement of the upcoming reunion thrummed through Maria's veins as she boarded the plane to Tampa. Gazing out the window at the cotton-ball clouds drifting by, she replayed her conversations with Regina and Cathy in her mind. Their unwavering support filled her with a sense of optimism. Finally, after a seemingly short flight, the announcement for landing in Tampa crackled through the speakers. As Maria disembarked, she spotted a familiar face waving from the baggage claim crowd. It was Paula, a radiant smile illuminating her features.

"Maria!" Paula called out, her voice brimming with warmth. Maria hurried towards them, the joy of their reunion washing away any lingering travel fatigue.

"Paula!" Maria exclaimed, pulling her cousin into a tight embrace. "It's so good to finally see you again in person!"

As they piled into Paula's minivan, the conversation flowed easily. Paula described their Thanksgiving Day traditions, a delightful blend of Filipino and American customs.

"We go to church in the morning, then prepare a traditional turkey feast for lunch," Paula explained. "And in the afternoon, we have a big karaoke party! The kids love it."

"Oh, I love karaoke too!" Maria exclaimed, her worries fading away as she connected with her cousin and her family. "Thanksgiving is tomorrow, right?"

"Yep!" Paula confirmed. "We go all out here in Florida. You're in for a treat."

The drive to Paula's house revealed a comfortable, three-bedroom, two-story dwelling. Stepping inside, Maria was greeted by the warm sight of a man with a kind smile, Victor, Paula's husband. Beside him stood three curious faces—Jade, Emil, and Zurich, their children, their eyes wide with anticipation.

"Maria, this is my husband, Victor," Paula beamed, gesturing towards the man with a warm smile and a kind twinkle in his eyes.

"It's a pleasure to finally meet you, Maria," Victor said, extending a hand. "Paula's told me so much about you."

"The pleasure's all mine, Victor," Maria replied, shaking his hand.

Maria's heart melted at the sight of the kids. "Hi there," she greeted, crouching down to their level. "I'm Maria, your aunt from North Carolina."

The children, initially shy, warmed up to Maria's gentle smile. Jade, the eldest, offered a tentative grin. Emil, full of boundless energy, bounced on his toes, eager to play. Zurich, the youngest, peeked at Maria from behind Paula's leg, his thumb in his mouth.

The afternoon unfolded in a flurry of activity. Paula bustled around the kitchen, prepping ingredients for the Thanksgiving feast, while Victor entertained the kids with stories. Maria, eager to contribute, offered her help with the *sisig*, the family's dinner.

"Are you sure, Maria?" Paula asked, her brow furrowed slightly. "You just got here, and you must be tired from the flight."

"Nonsense!" Maria insisted, a playful smile on her face. "Besides, who better to make *sisig* than someone who learned from the best?"

Paula chuckled, her initial hesitation melting away. "Alright, alright. But promise me you won't overdo it."

Maria readily agreed, donning an apron and diving into the task with practiced ease. The rhythmic chopping of onions and the sizzling of garlic in hot oil filled the kitchen with a familiar aroma, instantly transporting Maria back to her time in Papua New Guinea. It wasn't her mother's kitchen that came to mind, but the lively cooking lessons with Christine, her dear friend. Christine, with her infectious laugh and unwavering patience, had taught Maria the secrets of *sisig*, a dish that embodied the spirit of Filipino cuisine.

As Maria worked, she shared stories about her life back in North Carolina, a touch of wistfulness tinging her voice as she recounted familiar places and routines. Paula listened intently, occasionally interjecting with questions and advice. The conversation flowed seamlessly, punctuated by bursts of laughter from the living room where Victor kept the kids entertained.

By the time the aroma of sizzling *sisig* wafted through the house, the afternoon sun was casting long shadows outside. Maria presented the dish with a flourish, the glistening pork nestled on a bed of chopped onions and chili peppers.

"Wow, Maria, it looks amazing!" Paula exclaimed, her eyes widening in appreciation. The kids, drawn by the enticing aroma, crowded around the counter, their eyes glued to the sizzling masterpiece.

As everyone dug into it, compliments flowed freely. Maria beamed with pride, her heart full of gratitude for the warmth and acceptance she found. In that moment, surrounded by loved ones,

Maria knew this was just the beginning of a brighter future, a future brimming with the promise of family, love, and delicious *sisig*.

Chapter 53: Rollercoasters and a Sprinkle of Magic

The Florida sun beat down on Maria's face as she held her phone, a wide grin splitting her cheeks. "You won't believe the beach yesterday, Mama," she gushed, describing the white sand and turquoise waters of Sarasota in vivid detail. "Paula and Victor even taught me how to build a sandcastle that didn't wash away with the first wave!"

Her mother's laughter crackled through the receiver. "Sounds idyllic, Maria. But tell me all about your big theme park adventure today!"

Maria's excitement bubbled over. "It's been incredible, Mama! You wouldn't believe it, but Universal Studios is a whole other world. I rode the Jurassic Park River Adventure, and let me tell you, getting drenched by a T-Rex is quite the experience!"

They chatted for a while longer, Maria recounting the thrills and spills of her solo day at Universal Studios. She described the heart-stopping drops of the Incredible Hulk Coaster and the immersive world of The Wizarding World of Harry Potter, where she savored a Butterbeer and felt a pang of longing for her family and Raj by her side.

Suddenly, her father's face popped up on the screen. "Hey there, sweetheart," he greeted, his voice warm with affection. "How's the Sunshine State treating you?"

"Amazing, Papa!" Maria exclaimed, swiveling the camera to showcase the bustling Main Street of Disney's Magic Kingdom. Magical music filled the air, and the iconic Cinderella Castle loomed majestically in the distance. "This place is like stepping into a fairytale!"

They spent the next hour exploring the wonders of Disney virtually. Maria's family gasped in delight as she took them on a whirlwind tour—the whimsical rides, the colorful characters, and the delectable Mickey-shaped ice cream. They marveled at the meticulous details of the park, the vibrant parades, and the sheer joy radiating from the faces of families around them.

But first, Maria had to rewind a bit. "Oh, and before I forget," she began, "Thanksgiving was amazing! Paula went all out with a traditional turkey feast, but the real star of the show was the never ending karaoke, of course!" She chuckled at the memory, her parents' faces lighting up.

They spent a good chunk of the call reminiscing about Thanksgiving dinner, Maria recounting the warmth of Paula's family and the delicious food. Then, she seamlessly transitioned to the magic of Disney, sharing her experiences with the same enthusiasm.

As the sun dipped below the horizon, painting the sky in a dazzling array of orange and pink hues, Maria led her parents to a prime spot for the nightly fireworks display. A gasp escaped their lips as the first bursts of light filled the sky, illuminating Cinderella Castle with a shimmering glow.

"It's beautiful," her sister Lucy whispered, her voice filled with awe.

Maria, her heart brimming with magic and warmth, shared the experience not just with her parents but with Raj as well. With a quick tap on her phone, she added him to the video call.

A moment later, Raj's face appeared on the screen, a wide smile breaking across his features. "Hey there, beautiful! What a view!" he exclaimed, his voice filled with excitement.

"Isn't it?" Maria replied, her smile mirroring his. "Just wait till you see the fireworks!"

The call expanded to a four-way conversation as Raj greeted Maria's parents warmly. They exchanged pleasantries as they marveled at the dazzling display together.

As the final burst of fireworks faded, painting the night sky in a shower of glittering sparks, Maria ended the call with a bittersweet smile. The day had been filled with thrilling adventures and the comforting glow of family, both near and far. The pang of loneliness for her family and Raj's physical presence remained, but it was softened by the warmth of their virtual connection and the shared magic of the moment. The memory of this night, filled with laughter and the spectacle of Disney, would stay with her, a beacon of hope for the future.

Chapter 54: The Unseen Threat: A Summer Dream Deferred

March winds whipped through the open windows of Regina's kitchen, carrying the scent of simmering adobo and the chatter of family. Maria leaned back in her chair, a contented sigh escaping her lips.

Regina chuckled, stirring the stew. "Wow, time flies! Remember that first year feeling, the one right before you conquered your own classroom?"

Maria chuckled. "And stressed out of my mind, wondering if I'd even make it a semester."

"You were," Patrice chimed in, a playful glint in his eye. "But you know what they say, what doesn't kill you makes you tougher."

Maria grinned. "Something like that. But honestly, it's all thanks to you guys. Your support and encouragement kept me going."

Cathy piped up from across the table. "Yeah, you're practically a superhero now!"

Maria ruffled his hair affectionately. "Just a regular girl who learned a thing or two about perseverance."

Nestled comfortably in her bed, the afterglow of a delicious dinner with her friends lingering on her tongue, Maria reached for her phone. The warmth of her childhood room and the soft lamplight cast a comforting glow on her face. Tonight, something more than the usual contentment filled her. It was the excitement of sharing news that had been brewing since dinner.

As the faces of her parents filled the screen, Maria couldn't help but smile. "So, Mama, Papa," she began, "I've been thinking about summer..."

Her mother's eyes lit up. "Planning any exciting adventures?"

"You could say that," Maria replied, a smile tugging at her lips. "I'm actually close to booking a flight back to the Philippines!"

A chorus of gasps and excited chatter filled the room. Her sister Lucy squealed with delight. "Really, *Ate*? That's amazing!"

"We miss you, *Ate*," Miguel added, his voice filled with longing.

Maria's heart swelled with love for her siblings. "I miss you guys too, more than words can say. And of course, I can't wait to see you all again."

Her father's cleared his throat, a serious expression crossing his face. "That's fantastic, Maria. But have you considered the cost of the flight and your living expenses while you're there?"

Maria nodded, her smile unwavering. "I've been saving up diligently, Papa. I've got enough to cover everything."

Her mother's eyes welled with pride. "Our responsible Maria. We're so proud of you, *anak*."

The conversation flowed late into the night, filled with anticipation and plans for Maria's summer visit. They discussed potential adventures, long-overdue family gatherings, and the joy of simply being together again.

Little did they know, the world was teetering on the brink of a monumental shift. Just as Maria's summer dreams solidified, an invisible enemy began to cast a long shadow.

In the third week of March, a news alert flashed across Maria's phone screen, sending a jolt through her system: Global Lockdown Imposed Due to COVID-19 Pandemic. Fear gripped her heart as she read about the rapidly spreading virus and the unprecedented measures being taken to contain it.

The news hit them like a tidal wave. Maria's dream of a Philippine summer vanished, replaced by a chilling uncertainty. Her carefully laid plans crumbled before her eyes, leaving a void of disappointment and worry.

With a trembling voice, Maria dialed her family. Their usually cheerful greetings were replaced with hushed tones and worried questions. They shared stories of empty streets, overflowing hospitals, and a growing sense of fear gripping their community. Despite the miles separating them, the weight of the impending crisis hung heavy in the air. As the call ended, a tear rolled down Maria's cheek. The dream of a carefree summer had evaporated, replaced by a fierce determination to protect herself and her loved ones from the unseen threat that loomed large.

Chapter 55: A Daring Decision

April 2020. Spring's promise of renewal felt like a cruel joke in a world choked by the invisible grip of the pandemic. Schools were shuttered, streets eerily quiet, and the once vibrant tapestry of life had faded to a muted gray. A video call with her family in the Philippines on Easter Sunday only amplified Maria's sense of isolation. Their faces, framed by the glow of their laptops, mirrored her own longing.

The call took an unexpected turn when Leah, her American cousin from California, appeared on the screen. Years had passed since their last conversation, but the warmth in Leah's voice instantly bridged the gap. "Happy Easter, Maria!" she chirped, her smile a beacon of light in the gloom. "Since you can't get to the Philippines," she continued, "what about you coming to California this summer instead?"

Maria's heart lurched. The idea of escape, of adventure, was intoxicating. Yet, the world outside was a minefield of risk. Vaccines were still months away, and every cough, every touch, held the potential for disaster. But the chance to reconnect with a long-lost relative, someone she'd only known through stories, was a powerful draw.

Sensing Maria's hesitation, Leah offered a lifeline. "We'd be extra careful, of course," she promised. "Masks, sanitizer, everything we can do to stay safe. It wouldn't be the California you might have imagined, but it could be an adventure nonetheless."

The prospect of a unique adventure during a global lockdown resonated with Maria. Witnessing the world on hold, humanity grappling with an invisible enemy, could be a powerful experience. Taking a deep breath, she surprised even herself by saying, "Alright, *Ate*. Let's do this."

The excitement in Leah's voice was infectious. Plans were quickly hatched, flights booked with stringent safety protocols in mind. Now, Maria had to face a different challenge: telling her father.

The phone call was a mix of emotions. Her father, while genuinely happy for Maria's chance to reconnect with family, couldn't hide his worry. "California, Maria?" he asked, his voice laced with concern.

"I know, Papa," Maria replied, her own voice trembling slightly. "It sounds crazy, right? But this is *Ate* Leah, my cousin! And she's promised we'll be super careful."

A sigh escaped her father's lips. "Alright, *anak*," he finally conceded, the love for his daughter outweighing his fears. "Just promise me you'll be extra cautious, ckay? Double down on those precautions Leah mentioned. And call me every day, no excuses."

A wide smile spread across Maria's face. This trip was more than just an adventure. With newfound determination, she hung up the phone, ready to navigate the uncertainties of travel in a pandemic-stricken world. California awaited, promising not just sunshine, but a unique opportunity to witness human resilience in the face of an unprecedented crisis

Chapter 56: The Journey to Hayward

"Welcome to California!" a cheerful voice called out over the hum of travelers and the soft announcements echoing through the terminal.

Maria smiled behind her mask, adjusting the strap of her carry-on bag as she stepped out into the cool air of San Francisco International Airport. The airport was bustling, yet there was a palpable sense of caution. People moved purposefully, maintaining a respectful distance, faces mostly hidden behind masks. Signs reminding travelers to use hand sanitizer and practice social distancing were everywhere, a constant reminder of the ongoing pandemic.

Just outside the terminal, Maria spotted Leah waving enthusiastically next to a sleek, midnight-blue Tesla. Leah's husband, Brent, stood by, loading Maria's luggage into the trunk.

"Maria!" Leah called out again, her eyes crinkling into a smile above her mask.

Maria quickened her pace, her heart lightened by the familiar sight of her cousin. Leah enveloped her in a quick, warm hug, mindful of the times, before pulling back to introduce Brent.

"Brent, this is Maria. Maria, meet Brent, my better half," Leah said with a chuckle.

"Nice to finally meet you, Maria," Brent said, extending a hand which Maria shook firmly.

"Likewise, *Kuya* Brent. Thank you both for picking me up," Maria replied, her eyes shining with gratitude.

As they settled into the plush seats of the Tesla, Maria marveled at the smooth, quiet ride. The streets of San Francisco slipped by, a blend of historic charm and modern vibrancy, though noticeably subdued with fewer pedestrians and masked faces peeking out from every direction.

"So, how's everything in California?" Maria asked, looking out at the rows of picturesque houses as they crossed the Bay Bridge.

"We're managing," Leah said, turning slightly in her seat. "It's been strange, honestly. People are out and about, but there's always this undercurrent of caution. Masks, sanitizer, and social distancing are part of our daily routine now."

Brent nodded. "And working from home has become the norm for many. We've been trying to make the most of it, though. Like our new house in Hayward. You'll see, it's spacious enough for all the time we've been spending indoors."

Maria raised an eyebrow. "I can't wait to see it. A six-bedroom house, you said? That's incredible!"

Leah beamed. "We're very blessed. It felt like the right move, especially now that everything is so unpredictable."

Soon, they arrived in Hayward, and Maria couldn't hide her amazement as they pulled up to a beautiful, sprawling house nestled in a quiet neighborhood. The house was modern, with large windows and a welcoming façade that seemed to invite Maria inside.

"Welcome to our humble abode," Brent said, opening the door for Maria.

As Maria stepped inside, she took in the airy, sunlit rooms and the tasteful decor that spoke of Leah's meticulous eye for detail.

"Wow, *Ate*, this is beautiful," Maria said, her voice tinged with awe. "You've really done well for yourselves."

Leah's eyes softened as she looked around. "I was praying about whether to invite you over, especially with the pandemic and all. But I felt like I got a sign from my dad, your Uncle Ding. I believe he's my guardian angel now. It felt like he was nudging me to reach out to you."

Maria's eyes glistened with tears. "Thank you, *Ate* Leah. It means a lot to be here."

Leah smiled and reached out to touch a small, ornate urn on a nearby shelf. "This is where Dad's ashes are. And Mom's too. They're always with me."

Maria nodded, feeling a wave of emotion. "I'm sure they're watching over us."

She pulled out her phone and dialed her father. "Papa, I'm here. *Ate* Leah and *Kuya* Brent just showed me their beautiful new home."

Leah leaned in and waved at the phone. "Hi, *Tito*! Your daughter's in good hands."

Maria's father's voice crackled through the speaker, filled with warmth. "Thank you, Leah. I'm glad Maria has you both there."

Later that evening, Leah invited her older sister, Cora, who lived in San Francisco, to join them for dinner.

Maria greeted her cousin warmly as she arrived. "*Ate* Cora! It's been too long."

Cora embraced Maria. "It has, indeed. I'm so glad we could all get together tonight."

The dinner table was a lively mix of laughter and stories, punctuated by delicious dishes that Brent and Leah had lovingly prepared.

The night stretched on, filled with the warmth of family and the comfort of being together, even in uncertain times. As Maria looked around the table, she felt a deep sense of gratitude for Leah's invitation and the unseen guidance that had brought her here.

"Here's to family," Maria said, raising her glass. "And to the signs that lead us to where we need to be."

Chapter 57: Exploring the Heart of California

"California, here we come!" Maria thought as she gazed out of the car window, watching the cityscape of Hayward give way to the sprawling tech campuses and iconic landmarks she had long dreamed of visiting.

Leah's excitement was palpable as they set off towards the world-renowned Silicon Valley, the epicenter of innovation and technology. They started with a visit to the closed Apple headquarters at Apple Park in Cupertino. The sleek, futuristic design of the campus stood quiet and impressive under the California sun, a stark contrast to its usual bustling activity.

"Even though it's closed to visitors, just being here is amazing," Leah said, her voice filled with admiration.

They parked near the colossal circular building known as the "spaceship" at Apple Park. The sleek, futuristic design stood in stark contrast to the quiet, empty campus.

"This place is usually buzzing with activity," Brent explained. "It feels strange to see it so quiet."

Maria nodded, snapping a photo and sending it to her family group chat with a quick message: "At Apple HQ! Even closed, it's impressive!"

Their next stop was Facebook's Menlo Park campus. The iconic "thumbs up" sign was perfect for another photo opportunity.

"Say 'like'!" Cora joked, holding up her phone for a group selfie.

"Like!" Maria and Leah chimed in unison, grinning broadly behind their masks.

As they continued their tech tour, the Googleplex in Mountain View loomed large with its colorful bikes and whimsical architecture. Although tours were suspended, Maria couldn't resist capturing the playful vibe in her photos.

"Google has such a fun campus," Maria said, sending more pictures to Raj, her best friend back home. "Wish you were here to see this!"

The next day, Maria awoke with a thrill of anticipation for their San Francisco adventure. Leah and Brent drove her to the city, their first stop: the Golden Gate Bridge.

"Or should I say the Golden Gate," Maria quipped, learning its true name. The bridge's famous orange-red towers pierced the sky, framed by the bay's sparkling blue waters.

"Breathtaking, isn't it?" Brent said as they walked across part of the bridge, the wind whipping around them.

Maria nodded, the view capturing her completely. She took out her phone to capture the scene, tagging it with, "Golden Gate Bridge—Simply Stunning!"

Next, they wound their way to Lombard Street, the "Crookedest Street in the World." The steep, winding road was lined with beautiful, blooming flowers.

"This is so much fun!" Maria laughed as they slowly drove down, the curves making her feel like she was on a gentle rollercoaster.

From the bottom of Lombard Street, they had a view of the Ghirardelli Square, where Maria bought a chocolate gift pack.

"And there's Alcatraz," Leah pointed out, as they stood at the edge of the street, looking out over the bay.

"Even from a distance, it looks so haunting," Maria murmured, snapping a picture.

Later in the week, it was Cora's turn to play tour guide amid the ongoing pandemic. They began their day at her cozy one-bedroom condo in the heart of San Francisco.

"Welcome to my little slice of the city," Cora said warmly, guiding Maria through her neatly decorated space. The view from her window offered a panorama of the bustling city below, with Twitter's headquarters visible across the street. Despite the masked faces on the sidewalks below, it almost didn't feel like a pandemic at all.

"You have such a charming home, *Ate* Cora," Maria admired. "It's so quintessentially San Francisco."

Their exploration commenced with a visit to Oracle Park, home of the San Francisco Giants.

"This place is usually electric on game days," Cora reminisced as they walked past the quiet stadium.

Next, they wandered to Levi's Plaza, where the Levi Strauss & Co. headquarters are located.

"This is where the iconic jeans were born," Cora explained with a smile. "Pretty cool, right?"

They continued their journey to Chase Center, the new home of the Golden State Warriors.

"Wow, this is impressive!" Maria exclaimed, standing outside the arena. She quickly snapped a photo and sent it to her family. "Exploring more of SF with *Ate* Cora!"

Their day unfolded at Fisherman's Wharf, where they soaked in the bustling atmosphere, savored the aroma of fresh seafood, and watched tourists navigating the vibrant scene despite the ongoing pandemic.

"Fisherman's Wharf is such a sensory overload," Maria remarked, her eyes wide with wonder as they passed the vibrant shops and eateries.

At Pier 39, they watched the famous sea lions lounging and barking on the docks.

"They're adorable!" Maria giggled, capturing moments of the playful animals on her camera.

On their final day of adventure, Cora and Maria headed to Napa Valley for a day of wine tasting. The vineyards stretched out in rolling green waves under the Californian sun. Maria couldn't help but be surprised to find wine tasting venues open and people enthusiastically visiting them amidst the challenges of COVID-19

"This place is like a painting," Maria sighed as they sipped on fine wines, enjoying the serene beauty of the landscape.

"Cheers to good times and great company," Leah toasted, clinking her glass against Maria's. "I'm so glad you're here."

Maria smiled, feeling deeply grateful. "Me too, *Ate* Cora. This trip has been wonderful."

She took another photo of the vineyard and sent it to Raj, adding a caption: "Living the dream in Napa Valley with *Ate* Cora!"

The journey through California had been a series of unforgettable moments. From the quiet majesty of tech giants to the iconic beauty of San Francisco, and the tranquil allure of Napa Valley, Maria felt her heart full with memories. Every place had left its mark, each visit a thread woven into the fabric of her Californian adventure.

Maria returned home with a heart full of memories and a camera roll filled with snapshots of California's beauty. Each place they visited had left its mark, weaving together a tapestry of experiences that would stay with her forever.

Chapter 58: A Teacher's Journey Through a Pandemic

The world had become a sterile ballet of masked faces and social distancing. The vibrant energy of in-person classrooms Maria had dreamt of as a teacher had been replaced by the sterile glow of her laptop screen. August brought a return to the school building, but it was a ghost town of sanitized surfaces and minimal staff interaction. The joy of teaching was dampened by the empty desks and the disembodied voices of her students on the other side of the screen.

Back in North Carolina, Maria navigated these challenges with resilience and determination. Despite the stark differences from her initial dreams of teaching, she found solace in knowing that each day brought new opportunities to inspire her students, whether through a screen or in person.

One afternoon, while on her way home from school, Maria saw her landlords, Lita and Danny, in their closed transparent window. Both wore masks, their usual warm smiles muffled behind the blue fabric. Lita and Danny waved their hands for a friendly greeting. Her conversations with them were mostly concerned with checking in on Maria via video calls and making sure everything was alright and vice versa.

"Hey there, Maria," Lita greeted. "You look a little down. How's online teaching treating you?"

Maria sighed, rubbing her temples. "It's…different, to say the least. I miss the classroom energy, the connection with the students."

Danny chuckled, a hint of nervousness in his voice. "We all miss the old normal, honey. This pandemic has thrown everything for a loop. Heard about this new vaccine they're working on though? Sounds promising."

A flicker of hope ignited in Maria's eyes. "Really? That would be amazing!"

"Yeah, they're still in trials, but hopefully, it'll be the light at the end of the tunnel," Lita added, her voice laced with cautious optimism.

Later that evening, a video call connected Maria with Raj, his face creased with concern as he mirrored her mask-wearing attire.

"Hey, beautiful," Raj greeted, his voice laced with worry. "You seem troubled. What's on your mind?"

Maria poured out her anxieties—the fear for her family back home, the uncertainty of the future, the strange disconnect from her students. Tears welled up in her eyes as she spoke of the weight of the pandemic. After returning from her trip to California, Maria found herself grappling with renewed anxiety, compounded by the challenges of the ongoing crisis.

Raj listened patiently, his gaze unwavering. "It's okay to be scared, Maria. This is a scary time for everyone. But you're strong, and you're not alone in this. We'll get through it, together."

His words, a balm to her soul, brought a shaky smile to Maria's lips. They spent the rest of the call reminiscing about happier times, a shared anchor in the storm of uncertainty.

As December arrived, a sliver of hope pierced the oppressive gloom. News of the first COVID-19 vaccine receiving Emergency Use Authorization spread like wildfire. A wave of relief washed over Maria. Teachers, categorized as essential workers, would be among the first to receive the vaccine.

A glimmer of light flickered in the distance. Perhaps, just perhaps, the world could return to a semblance of normalcy. The invisible enemy might not be vanquished yet, but with the vaccine as a weapon, humanity had a fighting chance. The future, though still uncertain, held a promise—a promise of classrooms filled with laughter, of hugs shared with loved ones without fear, of a world reborn.

Chapter 59: The World Won't Wait

March 2021. The world was still emerging from the pandemic's shadow, but a spark of hope flickered in Maria's eyes. She'd received her first dose of the Pfizer vaccine the previous week, and a sense of cautious optimism filled her. School had transitioned to a "blended learning" model, with students attending in person every other day while others opted for online classes. This newfound flexibility allowed Maria to take a brief leave and embark on a long-awaited journey: renewing her Philippine passport in Washington DC.

Her two-day adventure began with a comfortable Amtrak ride from North Carolina. Sunlight streamed through the expansive windows, casting a warm glow over the passing scenery. Lush green fields stretched out as far as the eye could see, dotted with charming towns and quaint farmhouses. Occasionally, the rhythmic clickety-clack of the train was interrupted by the announcement of an upcoming station, each stop promising a new chapter in the unfolding landscape. As the train snaked its way north, Maria pulled out a book, the gentle rocking of the train a soothing lullaby for a focused reading session. Every now and then, she'd steal a glance out the window, mesmerized by the ever-changing tapestry of rural America.

The two-day trip flew by in a comfortable blur. Arriving in Washington DC, Maria wasted no time. Despite her short stay, she dove headfirst into the city's rich history and iconic landmarks. The towering Washington Monument, a beacon of white marble piercing the sky, filled her with awe. She wandered through the vast halls of the Smithsonian museums, each room a treasure trove of knowledge and artifacts. The solemn beauty of the Lincoln Memorial resonated with her, a powerful reminder of the nation's past struggles.

Traveling alone, once a source of apprehension, had become a liberating experience for Maria. She reveled in the freedom to set her own pace, to explore at her own whim. Video calls with Raj became her anchor, a way to share her experiences and connect with him despite the physical distance.

That day, as she stood on the steps of the Lincoln Memorial, the setting sun casting an orange hue across the reflecting pool, Maria dialed Raj's number. His face filled the screen, a mix of amusement and concern in his eyes.

"Hey, Maria! How's the political heart of America treating you?" Raj asked, a playful smile tugging at the corners of his lips.

Maria laughed, the sound echoing through the vast emptiness of the memorial grounds. "It's amazing, Raj! So much history packed into every corner. I feel like I'm walking through a textbook come to life."

"Sounds like you're having a blast exploring solo," Raj remarked, his voice laced with a hint of pride. "Are you getting used to it?"

"More than getting used to it," Maria admitted, a newfound confidence in her voice. "I'm actually kind of enjoying it! There's a real sense of freedom in setting my own itinerary and exploring at my own pace."

A pause settled between them, filled with the quiet hum of the city in the background.

"So, where to next, intrepid explorer?" Raj finally asked, a hint of curiosity in his voice.

Maria's eyes sparkled with excitement. "Guess what? My Easter adventure is going to be in the Big Apple itself—New York City!"

A wave of pride washed over Raj. "Maria, that's incredible! You're really getting the hang of this solo travel thing, aren't you?"

Maria beamed. "Absolutely! It's liberating, setting my own pace and exploring hidden gems. Sure, I miss having you by my side, but this pandemic won't stop me from conquering the world, one adventure at a time." The world wouldn't stop for her dreams, her aspirations. After all, her program had a time limit - five years, a finite window to explore. Who knew when this pandemic would truly end? Though she yearned for a world free from restrictions, a world where travel wouldn't be a solitary act, Maria wouldn't let it hold her back. With a newfound confidence and a heart full of wanderlust, she was determined to make the most of her remaining time. The Big Apple awaited, and beyond that, countless other destinations beckoned. The world was her oyster, and Maria was ready to explore it, bite by delicious bite.

Chapter 60: Concrete Jungle Where Dreams Take Flight

The sterile air of the airplane cabin was a stark contrast to the humid North Carolina spring Maria had left behind. Her fingers drummed a restless rhythm on the armrest, anticipation bubbling in her chest. As the plane descended, the iconic Manhattan skyline pierced the clouds, a jagged silhouette against the clear blue sky. This solo adventure was different—a whirlwind exploration of the Big Apple, a city pulsating with life even amidst the lingering shadow of the pandemic.

Stepping off the plane, Maria adjusted her face mask, a constant reminder of the new normal. Navigating the airport, she presented her vaccination ID with practiced ease, the document a passport to the city's vibrant tapestry.

Her first stop was Madame Tussauds, a haven of life-sized wax figures. Here, history and celebrity blurred. Masked and maintaining a safe distance, Maria marveled at the meticulous detail, snapping photos with her favorites—from a stoic Abraham Lincoln to a mischievous-looking Will Smith.

Next, she boarded a ferry to Liberty Island, the iconic Statue of Lady Liberty greeting her with a torch held high. The powerful symbol of freedom resonated deeply with Maria, a reminder of the struggles and triumphs that built this nation. Stepping onto Ellis Island, she could almost feel the echoes of immigrants who had passed through these very halls, their hopes and dreams breathing life into the city's fabric.

The following day, Maria decided to conquer the heights. Towering above the city, the Empire State Building offered breathtaking panoramic views. Wearing her mask, she joined a socially distanced queue, the wait punctuated by snippets of conversations in countless languages, a testament to the city's melting pot of cultures. Reaching the observation deck, she gasped at the vista sprawled before her—a concrete jungle teeming with life, a sea of skyscrapers stretching towards the horizon.

A short subway ride away awaited a unique architectural marvel—The Vessel, a honeycomb-like structure in Hudson Yards. Here, Maria marveled at the intricate steelwork, weaving her way up the different levels, her mask providing a sense of security in the close quarters. From the top, she enjoyed stunning views of the city and the nearby park.

Central Park, a sprawling oasis in the heart of the city, beckoned next. Removing her mask momentarily to take a deep breath of fresh air, Maria strolled along the tree-lined paths, the sounds of birdsong and laughter a welcome respite from the urban symphony. Street performers added their own artistic flair, their vibrant energy a testament to the city's unyielding spirit.

The vibrant chaos of Times Square was a sensory overload. Towering billboards flashed neon lights even through her mask, street performers jostled for attention, and the constant stream of humanity pulsed with an undeniable energy. Maria felt a surge of adrenaline, a thrill of being part of this ever-churning machine, even with the slight discomfort of the mask.

That evening, she indulged in the magic of Broadway, watching the timeless *"Phantom of the Opera."* Swept away by the soaring melodies and opulent costumes, she temporarily forgot the reality of the world outside. The mask remained, a necessary barrier, but it couldn't dim the sparkle in her eyes.

The somber mood of the 9/11 Memorial Museum offered a stark contrast. Walking through the exhibits, masked but deeply moved, Maria felt a deep sense of respect and sadness for those lost in the tragic attacks. The resilience of the human spirit, however, shone brightly through the displays of heroism and community.

No trip to New York City would be complete without indulging in its culinary delights. Maria savored everything from steaming hot dogs from street vendors, a delightful surprise after navigating a mask-muffled exchange, to melt-in-your-mouth pizzas in bustling restaurants. Each bite, enjoyed outdoors whenever possible for better ventilation, was a delicious adventure, a taste of the city's diverse culture.

Throughout her exploration, Maria stayed connected with loved ones back home. A video call with her family in the Philippines brought tears to her eyes. Their faces, filled with pride and joy, fueled her determination to discover more.

"New York is incredible, Mama!" Maria exclaimed, showing off the bustling scenery on her phone. "Even with the masks, everyone just seems so full of life!"

"We're so happy for you, Maria," her mother replied, her voice warm and loving. "Remember to stay safe and have fun!"

A separate call with Raj and his mother, Esha, was filled with laughter and shared stories.

"You're making us all jealous, Maria," Raj chuckled. "Sounds like you're getting the hang of this solo travel thing, even with the pandemic restrictions!"

"It's amazing, Raj," Maria replied, her smile wide. "I wish you were here to experience it with me."

"Don't worry, dear," Esha chimed in, her voice gentle. "There will be plenty of time for adventures together. But for now, enjoy this journey. You're making the most of it, mask and all!"

Maria's heart swelled with warmth. Despite the distance, she felt surrounded by love and support. These adventures, solo or not, were shaping her into a stronger, more independent woman.

The world was vast and exciting, and she wouldn't let anything, not even a pandemic, stop her from exploring it. One unforgettable masked experience at a time.

The remaining days in New York flew by in a whirlwind of activity. Maria explored vibrant neighborhoods like Chinatown and Little Italy, each with its own distinct flavor. She indulged in delectable dim sum and creamy gelato, the tastes a delightful explosion on her palate.

One evening, she splurged on a Michelin-starred dinner, a culinary journey unlike anything she'd ever experienced. The intricate presentation and explosion of flavors left her speechless. Even with her mask on, she couldn't help but let out a satisfied sigh with each bite.

The final leg of her adventure arrived with a visit to the Metropolitan Museum of Art. Here, she wandered through endless galleries, marveling at masterpieces from across the globe. From the haunting beauty of Egyptian mummies to the vibrant brushstrokes of Van Gogh, each piece transported her to a different world.

As she boarded the plane back to North Carolina, a bittersweet feeling settled over her. She was exhausted, yet exhilarated. New York City, with its relentless energy and captivating sights, had left an indelible mark on her soul. The constant presence of masks was a reminder of the pandemic's lingering shadow, but it couldn't dampen the spirit of the city or the spirit of adventure that now burned brightly within her.

Returning to the familiar routine of school life, Maria couldn't help but share her experiences with her students. They were captivated by her stories and pictures, transported to a world beyond their small town.

Chapter 61: Facebook Post 2

FAITH, HOPE AND LOVE.

When I was a child, I dreamed of traveling to the United States. Many years later, I not only got to travel, but I also found a teaching job in North Carolina, fulfilling a long-held aspiration.

As a little girl, I imagined visiting Disneyland. Decades later, I was thrilled to see Disney World in Florida, which is even grander than I ever imagined.

In my childhood, I dreamed of going to California and capturing a picture with the Golden Gate Bridge. Recently, I received a round-trip ticket to California and had the chance to explore San Francisco and its neighboring counties.

Washington, DC, and New York were also on my list of dream destinations. And now, in a short span of time, I have traveled to both of these iconic cities.

As the saying goes, no dream is too big, and no dreamer is too small. Keep chasing your dreams and trust in God's surprises. Remember, God's plans are always greater than our dreams.

Thank you, Lord! I owe everything to You!

#ToGodBeTheGlory

Chapter 62: A Shadow Falls

Emerging from the wooded trail, Maria took a deep breath, the crisp mountain air filling her lungs. Beside her, Regina stretched, a satisfied smile gracing her lips. "That was a lovely walk, Maria. Just what I needed to clear my head."

Maria returned the smile, a flicker of unease simmering beneath the surface. Earlier, during a video call with her mother, a forced cheer had masked a deeper concern.

"Happy Mother's Day, Mama!" Maria had exclaimed, waving her phone around to capture the vibrant scenery.

"*Salamat, anak!*" her mother beamed, a touch of surprise flickering in her eyes. "That's a beautiful place you're in."

"It is, Mama," Maria agreed, her heart swelling. "I just sent you a little something for Mother's Day."

A wave of gratitude washed over her mother's face. "Ten thousand pesos, Maria? You shouldn't have! You're working so hard already."

Just then, her father appeared on the screen, a tired smile etched on his face. "Hi *Tito*!" Regina chirped. "How are you?"

"I'm good, Regina," he rasped, his voice lacking its usual warmth.

Regina, ever the optimist, nudged Maria with a playful elbow. "Don't worry, *Tito*, Maria will double your present for Father's Day!"

Laughter erupted on the screen, but a shadow flickered in Maria's father's eyes, a fleeting sadness that sent a shiver down her spine. She brushed it aside, attributing it to her overactive imagination.

The following day, the phone call from her sister Lucy shattered the peace of Maria's weekend. "*Ate*," Lucy's voice trembled, "Papa... he hasn't been eating well."

Panic clawed at Maria's throat. "What do you mean? Did you take him to the doctor?"

"He doesn't want to go to the hospital, *Ate*," Lucy explained, her voice choked with worry. "They say everyone who goes in gets diagnosed with COVID. Mama and Miguel are insisting, but..."

"But what, Lucy? Can I talk to him?" Maria pressed, her heart hammering against her ribs.

A tense silence followed. "You can't talk to him right now," Lucy whispered finally. "They're still trying to convince him. They said they'll update you."

The news hung heavy in the air. The image of her father, his health seemingly deteriorating by the hour, filled Maria with a suffocating dread. Hours ticked by, each one an agonizing eternity. Finally, the call came—her mother's voice, strained and weary.

"Maria, your father... he's in the hospital. There was a long line in the emergency room, but they finally admitted him. Miguel is staying with him. I can't stay overnight, you know..." her voice trailed off, thick with emotion.

The unspoken truth crackled through the phone line. COVID. It had to be COVID. Panic clawed at Maria's throat. The news, a cruel confirmation of her worst fears, left her breathless. Her father, the strong, ever-reliable anchor of their family, confined within the sterile walls of a hospital battling a relentless disease.

As the enormity of the situation crashed over her, Maria felt a surge of helplessness, a desperate longing to be there, by his side. But the distance, a vast ocean separating them, mocked her desire.

With trembling hands, she closed the call, a single tear tracing a path down her cheek. The vibrant mountain scenery that had seemed so idyllic just moments ago now mirrored the turmoil within her. The weight of the unknown, the fear of the future, pressed down on her, a suffocating shroud.

Chapter 63: A Father's Last Gasp

The news hung heavy in the air, a suffocating weight Maria had carried since the call with Lucy. Her father, the pillar of their family, was battling COVID in the sterile confines of a hospital room. Miles away, she felt utterly helpless, a prisoner of distance and circumstance.

Back home, Lucy's voice, raspy with worry, crackled through the phone line. "*Ate*..." Her voice trailed off, the unspoken fear hanging heavy between them.

A cold dread gripped Maria. "Are you okay, Lucy?"

"Mama and I both tested positive," Lucy choked out, the tears threatening to spill over. "But we're praying for Papa, for all of us."

Maria's heart ached for her sister and mother, isolated and battling their own illness. The virus, a cruel thief, had stolen their health and their ability to be with their father during this critical time.

Later that day, a video call from Miguel brought a sliver of hope. He appeared on the screen, his face etched with worry and the telltale signs of his own illness. "*Ate*," he rasped, his voice rough, "Papa is not doing well. His oxygen levels are dangerously low."

Maria's breath hitched in her throat. The image of her father, a man of unwavering strength, fighting for each breath filled her with a suffocating dread. "Can I see him?" she pleaded.

Miguel hesitated, the stark white walls of the ICU stark against his grim expression. "He's not really himself right now, *Ate*. Maybe later." He held up his phone, revealing a glimpse of her father, his chest rising and falling with the help of a machine, a mask obscuring his face.

The sight was too much to bear. Tears welled up in Maria's eyes, blurring the image on the screen. "No," she choked out, "I can't."

The following days were a blur of agonizing silence and frantic updates from Miguel. Confined to their little home, Lucy and her mother clung to each other, their own illness adding another layer to their fear. Maria stayed glued to her phone, each ring a jolt of hope and terror in equal measure.

"He keeps asking for soda," Miguel reported one day, his voice heavy with concern. "But every time he tries to drink, he chokes."

Maria's heart ached for her father. Every detail, however small, painted a picture of his struggle. Then came the news that sent a fresh wave of terror crashing over them.

"The doctor wants to intubate him," Miguel explained, his voice tight with strain. "His oxygen levels are just dropping too low. It's the only way he can get enough air."

Maria gripped the phone so hard her knuckles turned white. The image of her father, a man who always seemed larger than life, reduced to a struggle for each breath, was a terrifying thought. "But..." she choked out, tears blurring her vision.

"I know, *Ate*," Miguel said, his own voice thick with emotion. "He wouldn't want this. But the doctor says without the tube, he..." he trailed off, unable to finish the sentence.

A heavy silence descended between them. Memories of their father's dislike for hospitals and machines filled Maria's mind. Yet, the thought of losing him altogether was unbearable.

"What do we do then?" she whispered, her voice barely audible.

Miguel sighed, the sound heavy with resignation. "We have to make a decision. It's either the tube or..."

Suddenly, a flurry of activity erupted on Miguel's end of the call. Muffled shouts and the frantic beeping of machines filled the air. Panic surged through Maria.

"Miguel! What's happening?" she cried, her voice rising in alarm.

The reply came a moment later, Miguel's voice barely a panicked whisper.

"His heart... his heart stopped, *Ate*! They're trying to revive him!"

Maria's breath hitched in her throat, replaced by a suffocating silence. Time seemed to stretch into an eternity as she listened to the faint sounds of frantic resuscitation efforts on the other end of the line.

Then, a miracle. A ragged gasp broke the silence, followed by the steady beep of a monitor. Relief washed over Maria, so intense it felt like a physical blow. Tears streamed down her face, a mixture of gratitude and terror. But the elation was short-lived.

After what felt like an eternity, Miguel called again. His voice, raw and shaky, sent a fresh wave of trepidation through Maria. She answered, her heart hammering against her ribs.

Silence stretched on the other end of the line, heavy and suffocating. Finally, Miguel spoke, a single word that shattered the fragile hope that had bloomed in Maria's chest.

"He's back," Miguel rasped, his voice choked with emotion. "They were able to revive him. But the doctor says he needs dialysis. Mama, Lucy and I... we decided against it."

Maria felt the floor drop from beneath her. Relief at his survival battled with the agonizing knowledge of the difficult choice they had made. Denial, a fleeting shield against the crushing weight of reality, threatened to engulf her. But a deeper truth resonated within her—her father was hanging by a thread.

In that moment of raw vulnerability, Maria turned to a source of strength that had always been a cornerstone of her family's life—faith. With trembling hands, she clasped them together, her gaze rising towards the heavens. A silent prayer, a desperate plea, escaped her lips. "Mary, Help of Christians," she whispered, her voice thick with emotion, "please protect my Papa. Hold him in your mantle, intercede for him with your Son. We surrender everything to you, God. Please, let him live." Tears streamed down her face, a mixture of gratitude and a renewed wave of fear clinging to the sliver of hope that remained.

Two agonizing hours passed before Miguel called again. This time, the silence on the other end of the line spoke volumes.

"*Ate*," his voice was barely a whisper, "Papa... he's gone."

The world dissolved into a blur of static. The phone slipped from Maria's grasp, clattering to the floor with a hollow thud. A choked sob escaped her lips, a single, desolate sound that echoed in the deafening silence of the room. The vibrant mountain vista outside her window mocked her with its cruel indifference. She was adrift in a sea of grief, a lone survivor clinging to a wreckage of shattered hopes. In that desolate expanse, a single, agonizing question echoed in the hollow chambers of her heart: would the fragile lifeline of their bond be strong enough to weather the storm that had ripped their world apart.

Chapter 64: Lost at Sea

The endless ribbon of highway blurred beneath Maria's tear-streaked eyes. Her hands, gripping the steering wheel with white-knuckled desperation, couldn't hold back the tremors that racked her body. Every sob that escaped her lips sounded like a fractured prayer, a broken plea for a miracle that never came. "Papa," she rasped, the word a desperate echo in the vast emptiness of the car.

News of her father's passing had hit her mother like a physical blow. The woman who had always been the pillar of strength had withered under the weight of grief, retreating into a chilling silence. It was Lucy, weakened by her own illness, who had delivered the news through choked sobs. Their cousin, Raymond, a beacon of kindness in a storm, had taken on the impossible task of handling the arrangements—the cremation, the paperwork, the suffocating burdens that threatened to break them.

But for Maria, miles away and bound by travel restrictions, helplessness was a constant companion. The ache in her chest was a living entity, a constant reminder of the distance that separated her from her family in their darkest hour. Virtual calls offered a cold comfort. Witnessing her mother's vacant eyes, the raw pain etched on Lucy's face, only intensified her own anguish.

Back in her lonely apartment, surrounded by the well-meaning gestures of friends who had started a novena for the dead, Maria found little solace. The murmured prayers, the flickering candles, felt like faint echoes in the deafening silence of her grief. Most of the time, she found herself curled up on the couch, the vibrant memories of her father a cruel mockery of their present reality.

Raj, her boyfriend, who had stayed by her side since the news of her father's illness, had tried to offer comfort. He'd call her periodically, his voice laced with concern, but his words felt like pebbles tossed into an ocean of grief. The world seemed to have lost its color, its vibrancy stolen by the absence of her anchor, the man who had always held their family together.

"Why us?" the silent question echoed endlessly in the hollow chambers of her heart. The injustice of it all, the cruel hand of fate that had snatched him away, threatened to consume her. But amidst the crushing grief, a flicker of despair extinguished any remaining determination. There was nowhere to go, no solace to be found.

Maria drove on, a lone figure lost at sea, her steering wheel a makeshift rudder against a tide of sorrow. The road stretched endlessly before her, a journey with no clear destination, a path leading only into the endless abyss of grief. She was adrift, unmoored, and utterly alone.

Chapter 65: Embers in the Ashes

Days bled into week, a monotonous blur of forced smiles and choked back tears for Maria. The vibrant colors of her life had leached away, replaced by a dull grey that mirrored the emptiness she felt within. The apartment felt suffocating, the silence punctuated only by the rhythmic tick of the clock, a constant reminder of time's relentless march forward while she remained trapped in her grief.

The insistent buzzing of her phone pierced the silence. It was Raj, his name flashing on the screen a beacon of warmth in the encroaching darkness.

"Maria?" His voice, laced with concern, washed over her like a gentle wave.

A choked sob escaped her lips. "Raj," she whispered, the sound raw and unfamiliar even to her own ears.

"Hey, it's okay," he soothed, his voice a balm to her frayed nerves. "Talk to me, what's going on?"

The dam broke. Words tumbled out in a torrent, a chaotic mix of grief, despair, and a suffocating sense of hopelessness. She confessed her fear of the future, the crushing weight of responsibility towards her siblings, and the overwhelming urge to simply sink beneath the tide of sorrow.

Silence hung heavy on the line for a moment, then Raj spoke, his voice firm yet gentle. "Maria, listen to me. It's okay to grieve, to feel lost. But you can't let it consume you. Your father wouldn't want that."

His words hit a nerve. A flicker of defiance ignited within her. "But how can I be strong for them, Raj? How can I be the pillar they need when I feel like I'm falling apart myself?"

"You don't have to be strong alone," Raj replied. "That's what family is for. Lean on your siblings, Maria. They need you, but you need them too. Together, you can find the strength to carry on, to honor your father's memory."

His words resonated deep within her. A spark, faint but persistent, flickered to life in the ashes of her despair. Yes, she was hurting. But she wasn't alone. She had her siblings, their shared memories, and the love that bound them together.

"You're right, Raj," she whispered, a newfound determination strengthening her voice. "I can't give up. I have to be strong for them, for myself."

"That's the Maria I know," Raj replied, his voice filled with quiet pride. "Remember, even the smallest embers can rekindle a fire. You'll get through this, Maria. I'll be here for you, every step of the way."

The call ended, but the embers of hope had been fanned. Maria wiped away her tears, a resolute glint in her eyes. She wouldn't let the grief paralyze her. For her father, for her siblings, and for herself, she would find the strength to rise from the ashes and embrace life once more. The road ahead would be long and arduous, but she wouldn't walk it alone.

Chapter 66: Signs from Beyond

"27,672.49 PHP. That's our late father's discounted hospital bills."

Maria stared at the figure on the hospital statement, her heart aching with a bittersweet resonance. The significance of the number was unmistakable. Her father was born on January 27, 1949, and passed away at the age of 72. And now, his interment was set for June 6. The alignment of these dates and numbers felt like a message from beyond, a whisper of his presence still entwined in their lives.

As Maria processed this, she couldn't help but ponder the mysteries of life and death. Did our deceased loved ones remain with us in some unseen way? This thought lingered in her mind, finding echoes in the peculiar occurrences she had experienced since her father's passing.

Every Sunday, Maria drove to mass, seeking solace and connection in her faith. One morning, after a particularly hot day, she parked her car and noticed something strange. Despite the sweltering heat, her car was covered in wet streaks, as if it had just been through a rainstorm, while every other car in the lot, including her landlords' vehicles, stood dry under the relentless sun.

Another time, following a torrential downpour, her car remained inexplicably dry, while all the others were soaked, glistening with raindrops. She stood there, beneath the gray sky, feeling a shiver run through her. Was it merely a coincidence, or was it a sign?

These anomalies left Maria pondering the mysteries of life and death. Did these peculiarities with her car hint at something deeper? She often thought back to the day she bought her car. She had wished then that her father could be her passenger, sharing in the joy of her new purchase. These oddities with her car seemed to hint that perhaps he was, in some mysterious way, still with her, riding along as her silent companion.

The signs didn't stop with the car. In their family's garden, a green butterfly had become a frequent visitor. Green was a deeply significant color for her father. It was the color of his favorite shirt, a shirt he wore often, and the color of the urn that now held his ashes. Her family noticed the butterfly and would often speak of it as a symbol of their father's presence, fluttering around them, bringing a sense of comfort and continuity.

As the days drew closer to her father's interment, Maria held onto these signs. They brought her a sense of peace amidst the grief. She cherished each encounter with the green butterfly, each puzzling moment with her car, seeing them as tender reminders of her father's enduring love and presence. Despite the sadness of his physical absence, Maria felt a deep connection to him, woven through these fleeting, yet profound, signs.

In those quiet moments of reflection, she believed more than ever that the bonds of love and family transcend even the boundaries of life and death.

Chapter 67: Stepping into Strength

Three days had crawled by since their father's interment. The days felt surreal, a hazy collage of whispered prayers and tear-stained visits to relatives. The sharp scent of lilies, a constant reminder of the funeral, still lingered in the air. Amidst this, a message from Lucy, her voice hoarse on the phone, relayed their gratitude to friends and family who had offered solace during the funeral.

That evening, with a deep breath that hitched in her throat, Maria gathered her family for a video call. Stepping into a role she hadn't quite anticipated, yet fiercely determined to embrace, she stared at the screen showing the familiar faces. Each face bore the raw marks of grief, etched in tear-rimmed eyes and drawn faces. The flickering screen cast a blue glow on Maria's tear-streaked face, highlighting the worry lines that had etched themselves deeper in the past week.

"Thank you all for joining," Maria began, her voice steady despite the tremor in her hand clutching the phone. "I know these past days have been a storm for all of us. Papa... well, Papa always told us to be strong, to be there for each other. He wouldn't want to see us drowning in sorrow. We need to be each other's anchors now."

Lucy's eyes welled up again, a single tear tracing a path down her cheek. But a resolute nod followed. "*Ate* is right. Papa wouldn't want us to be broken. We have to keep going, for him and for each other."

Miguel, leaned closer to the screen, his jaw set. "We have to live in a way that honors his memory. He always believed in us, even when we doubted ourselves. We owe it to him to carry on, to support each other, just like he would have done."

Their mother, spoke in a hushed voice. "It's hard to imagine life without his laugh echoing in this house, but we have to move forward. Together, we can do this."

Maria felt a surge of pride and determination course through her. "We've faced challenges before," she continued, the weight of responsibility settling on her shoulders yet strangely accompanied by a sense of clarity. "We are strong. We are resilient. We can't let this break us. We need to lean on each other, to find strength in the bond we share as a family. That's what Papa would have wanted."

The call ended with a renewed sense of purpose. Each family member, though burdened with grief, carried a flicker of hope. They were tethered together by shared memories, their collective love, and the unspoken promise to honor their father's legacy by living with strength and unity.

Maria closed her eyes, a single tear escaping her lashes. A memory surfaced: her father, his face etched with the lines of a life well-lived, his voice gentle yet unwavering, *"Always remember, Maria, even the strongest storms pass. And when the sun shines again, you'll find the strength to bloom anew."* She knew now, more than ever, that their roots ran deep, intertwined. Together, they would weather the storm.

Chapter 68: Glimmers of Hope

A year had passed since her father's passing. The world felt different, a strange mix of cautious optimism and lingering shadows of grief. The news was finally buzzing with positive developments —COVID-19 vaccines had become widely available across the globe, and the Philippines, along with many other countries, had begun a phased rollout. Relief washed over Maria as she watched her mother and siblings receive their first doses, a tangible step towards a future where the fear of the virus wouldn't be a constant companion.

However, normalcy seemed to return at a glacial pace. Schools were still hesitant to fully embrace face-to-face learning, opting for a hybrid' model that left Maria yearning for the pre-pandemic days when classrooms hummed with life. A pang of sadness hit her. "Papa would have loved to hear that the school is slowly coming back to life," she confided in Raj, her voice laced with a hint of melancholy during their evening call.

"He would be proud of you, Maria," Raj responded warmly. "You've shown incredible strength this past year. He wouldn't want you to dwell on the past. Focus on the future, on the new chapter this vaccine rollout opens up."

Raj's words offered solace, but a tinge of bittersweetness remained. His voice, usually filled with vibrant energy, seemed subdued. After a moment's hesitation, he spoke.

"Speaking of new chapters," he began, "I finally accepted a job as a finance consultant in the UK. *Maa* and I are thrilled!"

Maria's heart swelled with joy for him. "That's fantastic news, Raj! Congratulations! I knew you'd land your dream job."

"Thanks, love," Raj replied, his voice regaining its usual cheer. "*Maa*'s ecstatic. She can't wait to visit my brother in London. We've been planning a trip for months."

A smile spread across Maria's face. "That's wonderful! So, Esha *Maa* will be traveling back and forth?"

"Yeah," Raj chuckled. "She's already planning her three-month visa cycles between India and the UK."

Maria couldn't help but laugh. Memories of her own recent trip with friends resurfaced. "Speaking of travel," she said, "Remember my Virginia Beach trip with Patrice, Cathy, and Regina? We found a Jollibee there! You wouldn't believe how excited we were to gorge ourselves on spaghetti and *chicken joy*."

Laughter filled the air as they reminisced about their shared experiences, both past and future. While challenges remained, a renewed sense of hope permeated their conversation.

That evening, as the last rays of sunlight dipped below the horizon, Maria uttered a prayer of thanks. Gratitude for her family's health, the promise of normalcy on the horizon, and for Raj's exciting opportunity. "Thank you, Lord," she whispered, her voice thick with emotion. "Thank you for your blessings, Blessed Mother, and for your protection, St. Michael. You have carried us through this storm, and I trust that you will continue to guide us on the path to healing."

Chapter 69: Homecoming

The plane dipped its wing, revealing a breathtaking tapestry of emerald islands fringed with white sand beaches. A wave of excitement washed over Maria as she peered out the window. After two long years of travel restrictions, she was finally back in the Philippines, the vibrant colors and familiar warmth a balm to her soul. Beside her, Christine, nudged her arm, a wide grin splitting her face.

"Can you believe it, Maria? We're actually here!" Christine exclaimed, her voice buzzing with childlike enthusiasm.

Maria laughed, the sound rich with relief and joy. "Feels like forever, doesn't it? But hey, at least we made it."

Their friendship had endured the test of distance, their virtual catch-ups a lifeline during the long months of isolation. Now, they were eager to create new memories, their laughter echoing through the airplane cabin as they reminisced.

The plane finally touched down at Clark International Airport, the announcement met with excited chatter and the clatter of carry-on luggage.

Stepping off the plane and into the bustling airport, Maria was swept into a warm embrace by her mother. The familiar scent of her mother's perfume and the comforting warmth of her hug washed over her, erasing any lingering anxieties of the journey.

"*Anak*," her mother crooned, her voice thick with emotion. "It's so good to have you home!"

Joining the embrace were her siblings, Lucy and Miguel, their excited greetings creating a symphony of joy. Laughter and tears mingled as they held onto each other, a tangible expression of their love and relief at being reunited.

Their first stop was a visit to their father's grave. The cemetery, nestled amidst rolling hills, was a place of serene beauty. As they walked towards the familiar headstone, a wave of emotion washed over Maria. Tears welled up in her eyes as she knelt beside the grave, placing a bouquet of lilies on the cool marble surface.

"Hi Papa," she whispered, her voice trembling slightly. "I'm finally home. I wish you were here to see it."

Silence settled around them, broken only by the gentle rustling of leaves. Taking a deep breath, Maria shared stories of her travels with Christine, her voice gaining strength with each passing moment.

Her siblings exchanged knowing smiles, a silent reminder of shared memories and the bond that held them together. After spending a quiet moment at the grave, they said their goodbyes, leaving a piece of their hearts with their father.

Later that evening, Maria treated her friend Chu, a local, to dinner at a cozy restaurant tucked away in a bustling neighborhood. As they devoured plates of crispy *adobo* and steaming rice, their conversation flowed effortlessly.

"So, tell me all about your new job at the community center," Maria said, spearing a piece of glistening pork belly. "You sound so passionate about it."

Chu's eyes lit up with enthusiasm. "It's incredible, Maria! We're working with underprivileged kids, helping them with their education and after-school activities It's truly rewarding."

They spent the next few hours catching up, sharing stories, and laughing until their sides ached. As the night drew to a close, Maria felt a surge of gratitude for the unwavering support of her friends, a reminder of the importance of cherished connections.

The next few days were a whirlwind of activity. Maria and her family explored bustling markets, haggling for souvenirs with playful banter, and relaxed on pristine beaches, the turquoise water lapping gently at their toes.

One afternoon, while Maria and Christine were wandering through a bustling mall, Maria bumped into someone entirely unexpected.

"Franz?" she gasped, her heart skipping a beat as their eyes met. Franz, her former boyfriend from their Papua New Guinea days, stood before her, a flicker of surprise mirroring her own expression. The years seemed to melt away, leaving them suspended in a moment charged with unspoken emotions.

An awkward silence stretched between them, the weight of their past relationship hanging heavy in the air.

"Maria," Franz finally spoke, his voice a husky whisper. "It's... good to see you."

"You too," she replied, her voice barely above a murmur.

Christine, sensing the tension, nudged Maria's arm. "Hey guys, do you know each other?"

"Yes," Maria said, forcing a smile. "We met a few years ago in Lae."

Christine's eyes widened in recognition. "Oh wow, that's amazing! Small world, huh?"

Feeling the need for privacy, Maria suggested they find a quiet corner to chat. Christine, picking up on the unspoken cue, smiled apologetically.

"Well, I'll leave you two to catch up. I need to grab a coffee anyway. See you later, Maria?"

Maria nodded, a silent thank you in her eyes. As Christine disappeared into the throng of shoppers, Maria and Franz found themselves alone, the weight of their past pressing down on them.

Taking a deep breath, Maria broke the silence. "I... I wanted to apologize for how things ended between us," she said, her voice laced with regret.

Franz met her gaze, a mixture of surprise and vulnerability flickering in his eyes. "Apologize? But it was me who..." he trailed off, his voice laced with guilt.

"No, let me finish," Maria insisted, her voice gaining strength. "I shouldn't have run away like that. I should've talked to you."

A heavy silence descended upon them, broken only by the distant sounds of the mall. Finally, Franz spoke, his voice raw with emotion.

"And I should have been more understanding," he confessed. "My insecurities pushed you away."

A wave of relief washed over Maria. Hearing him acknowledge his part in their estrangement was a cathartic release.

"We were both young and scared," she said softly. "But I'm glad we could have this conversation now."

They spent the next hour talking, revisiting their memories of Papua New Guinea, both good and bad. They acknowledged their mistakes, expressed their regrets, and ultimately, found a sense of closure.

As they parted ways, a fragile peace settled between them. The spark they once shared might have flickered and died, but the embers of respect and understanding remained.

Maria walked out of the mall with a lighter heart. The reunion with Franz, though unexpected, had brought a sense of resolution. The journey home had been filled with laughter, tears, and unexpected encounters, but most importantly, it had been a journey of self-discovery and rediscovering the strength of her bonds with family and friends. As she hailed a taxi, a smile bloomed on her face. There was still so much to explore, so many memories to create, and she was ready to face it all, one adventure at a time.

Chapter 70: Seoul Searching

The brisk Seoul air swirled with anticipation as Maria and her family disembarked from the plane. Stepping into the bustling Incheon International Airport, they were greeted by a symphony of unfamiliar sounds—announcements in Korean, excited chatter, and the rhythmic melody of rolling luggage.

A mischievous grin spread across Maria's face. "Welcome to the Land of Morning Calm, everyone!" she exclaimed, her voice tinged with excitement.

Her siblings echoed her enthusiasm, their faces a mix of anticipation and nervous energy. The three-day trip to South Korea, a long-awaited dream finally coming true, promised a whirlwind of cultural immersion, delicious food, and unforgettable experiences.

However, this adventure wasn't just about exploring a new country; it was also a chance for Maria to introduce her family to Raj. He'd managed to snag a few days of leave from his new job in the UK and surprised Maria with a trip to Seoul.

"Welcome to the madness!" Maria chuckled, squeezing his hand reassuringly.

Raj offered her family his most charming smile. "*Annyeonghaseyo* everyone. It's so nice to finally meet you all in person."

"*Annyeonghaseyo!*" her siblings replied in unison, their faces beaming with curiosity.

The ice was broken. Over the next few hours, Maria's family readily took to Raj. His genuine warmth and playful banter with her siblings quickly put everyone at ease. Her mother, ever observant, watched the interaction with a knowing smile.

Their first stop was Gyeongbokgung Palace, a majestic complex adorned with intricate carvings and vibrant colors. Raj, ever the history buff, narrated fascinating tales of the Joseon Dynasty, captivating Maria's siblings and earning points with her mother.

"Wow, Raj! You know your stuff!" Miguel exclaimed, impressed by his knowledge.

As they strolled through the expansive courtyards, Raj couldn't resist playfully reenacting a scene from a historical Korean drama, much to the amusement of Lucy and her mother. Maria watched fondly, her heart brimming with happiness.

Their day continued with a visit to the lively Myeongdong shopping district, a labyrinth of bustling streets crammed with shops selling everything from traditional Korean hanboks to the latest K-Pop merchandise. Maria and her mother delighted in browsing colorful accessories, while Miguel, Lucy and Raj haggled good-naturedly with a street vendor over a souvenir keychain. Raj, ever the supportive boyfriend, helped Miguel secure the best deal, earning a grateful nod from the younger brother.

The highlight of their second day was undoubtedly a trip to N Seoul Tower, a towering landmark offering panoramic views of the sprawling cityscape. As they stood on the observation deck, the bustling city stretched out before them, a dazzling tapestry of lights and skyscrapers.

"This view is incredible," her mother whispered, her voice filled with awe.

Later that night, fueled by a delicious dinner of *bibimbap* and *bulgogi*, they decided to let loose at a local karaoke bar. Laughter filled the room as they took turns belting out their favorite Korean songs—from classic ballads to upbeat K-Pop hits. Raj, surprisingly turned out to be one of them, a karaoke star, belting out English songs with impressive accuracy and enthusiasm.

"We should definitely go to a karaoke bar in London, Raj!" Maria declared, wiping tears of laughter from her eyes.

"Absolutely," Raj replied, his voice slightly hoarse from singing. "Just promise you'll be my backup singer."

The night ended with a group photo booth session, their faces contorted into silly expressions captured in a strip of hilarious photos.

Back at their hotel, Maria watched from her window as the city lights twinkled below. Beside her, Raj wrapped his arm around her, a comfortable silence settling between them.

"I can't believe you're here with me," she whispered, leaning into his embrace. "This is perfect."

"Anything for you," Raj replied, placing a kiss on her forehead. "And besides, seeing you introduce me to your family was the real highlight."

A smile bloomed on Maria's face. This trip wasn't just about exploring a new country; it was about creating new memories and forging stronger bonds—both with her family and with the man she loved.

Chapter 71: Crossroads and *Merienda* Decisions

Time, a relentless tide, had swept Maria back to the familiar shores of North Carolina. The whirlwind of her South Korean adventure with Raj and his surprise visit faded into a cherished memory, yet the echoes of their conversation resonated within her. His suggestion to apply for jobs in the UK had planted a seed of desire—a longing to bridge the geographical distance that separated them.

Now, on the cusp of finishing her third year in the cultural exchange program, Maria found herself at a crossroads. The prospect of extending her stay for two more years, as initially planned, held less appeal than before. The program had enriched her life, broadened her horizons, but her heart yearned for something more—a future intertwined with Raj's.

One sunny afternoon, the enticing aroma of frying *lumpia* wafted through Maria's apartment door. A smile tugged at her lips. Lita, her ever-generous landlady, was famous for her surprise afternoon snacks, a delicious tradition that had become a highlight of their days.

Reaching for her phone, Maria sent a quick text. "Smells amazing! Can I come over for *merienda*?"

Moments later, Lita's reply buzzed back. "Of course! Come down whenever you're ready."

Maria joined Lita and Danny, in their cozy kitchen. The table was laden with a feast—golden *lumpia*, steaming cups of tea, and a plate of freshly sliced mangoes.

As they dug into the delicious spread, Maria felt a familiar warmth wash over her. Lita and Danny weren't just her landlords; they were her friends-turned-family, a constant source of support and laughter.

Lita, noticing a contemplative look on Maria's face, offered a gentle nudge. "Something on your mind?"

Taking a deep breath, Maria shared her dilemma. "It's about the program," she began, "I've been thinking a lot lately..."

Lita immediately sensed something was amiss. "Is everything alright, Maria? You seem troubled."

Maria poured out her heart, sharing the memories from South Korea and the lingering ache of being apart from Raj. The unspoken question hung heavy in the air—how could she build a future with him from across the ocean?

Lita listened patiently, her eyes filled with understanding. "Maria," she said gently, "we know how much this program has meant to you. But life also has a way of throwing curveballs, doesn't it?"

A flicker of doubt crossed Maria's mind. Leaving the program unfinished, the uncertainty of a job search in a foreign country—these were daunting prospects.

Sensing her hesitation, Lita offered a reassuring smile. "Don't be afraid to chase after what your heart desires," she said, her voice firm but kind. "You're a bright, capable young woman, Maria. We have no doubt you'll find your way."

Danny nodded in agreement. "And hey, if things don't work out exactly as planned, you know you have a home here or in the Philippines. We'll always be your biggest supporters."

Maria's heart swelled with gratitude. Their unwavering support was a balm to her anxieties. Taking a deep breath, she looked at them, her eyes shining with newfound resolve.

"You're right," she said, a smile gracing her lips. "I need to follow my heart. Thank you for everything. You have no idea how much your support means to me."

Lita and Danny exchanged a knowing smile. They couldn't shield Maria from the challenges that lay ahead, but they could offer her the comfort of a safe haven and the unwavering belief in her ability to navigate her own journey. As they sat around the table, the aroma of snacks mingling with the warmth of their conversation,

Maria knew one thing for certain: it was time to take a leap of faith, to chase after the love that awaited her across the ocean. The road ahead might be filled with challenges, but with the love and support of her friends-turned-family, she was ready to face them head-on.

Chapter 72: Journey's Edge

Maria had been yearning for a fresh start, and now, the possibility of teaching in the UK was within reach. After submitting her resume and all the necessary documents to a recruitment agency, she felt a spark of hope. Her excitement grew when she received a call for an initial interview. She requested references from Mr. Carter, her school principal, and Alice, the head of math department. Both were enthusiastic and supportive. Maria also prepared a video introduction, showcasing her teaching abilities and experiences.

One Tuesday afternoon, as she was wrapping up her day at school, an email notification lit up her phone. She quickly opened it, her heart pounding with anticipation.

Email from the Recruitment Agency:

Subject: Interview Opportunity

Dear Maria,

We are pleased to inform you that a school in London has expressed interest in interviewing you for a mathematics teaching position. Please let us know your availability for a Zoom interview this week.

Best regards,

UK Recruitment Team

Maria's eyes widened, and a smile spread across her face. She couldn't contain her excitement and immediately dialed Raj's number.

"Hey, beautiful!" Raj's voice crackled through the phone, warm and familiar.

"Raj! Guess what? I got an email from the recruitment agency. There's a school in London that wants to interview me!" Maria's voice was filled with excitement and disbelief.

"That's amazing, Maria!" Raj exclaimed. "I knew you could do it. This is just the beginning. Tell me everything! What's the school like?"

"I don't have all the details yet," Maria replied, her voice trembling with joy. "But it's in London, and they want to schedule a Zoom interview this week. I can't believe this is happening!"

Raj's laughter was infectious. "This is incredible news. If you get this job, we'll finally be together! I can't wait explore UK with you!"

Maria sighed with relief. "It feels surreal, Raj. I was so nervous about this whole process, but now… I'm actually excited. Just imagine us walking along the Thames or visiting the British Museum."

"It's going to be fantastic," Raj said reassuringly. "Just be yourself in the interview. They'll see how talented and passionate you are. Remember to highlight your experience and your adaptability, especially how you've handled teaching during the pandemic."

"Good point," Maria agreed, taking mental notes. "And I'll mention the new teaching strategies I've implemented. I just hope I can convey how much this opportunity means to me."

"You will, love," Raj said softly. "You've been amazing throughout this entire process. And just think, once you're here, we can start planning our future together. No more long-distance calls."

Maria felt a wave of warmth and hope wash over her. "I can't wait for that, Raj. It feels like a dream coming true. But…" she hesitated, her voice faltering slightly, "I've been getting these headaches lately. I think it's all the stress from job hunting and the uncertainty of everything."

Raj's voice was filled with concern. "I'm sorry to hear that, Maria. Make sure you're taking care of yourself. Try to relax and get plenty of rest. Your health is more important than anything else."

"I know, I know," Maria said, trying to sound reassuring. "I'll take it easy tonight. I'm just so eager for this next step."

"Promise me you'll rest," Raj insisted. "You need to be at your best for the interview. And if you need to talk or just want to relax, I'm always here for you."

Maria smiled, feeling the comfort of his words. "Thank you, Raj. I promise I'll rest. But for now, I should probably go. This headache is getting worse."

"Alright, love," Raj said gently. "Take care of yourself. And don't worry, everything's going to be fine. I believe in you."

"Thanks, Raj. I'll talk to you later. Love you."

"Love you too, Maria. Get some rest and dream about London."

As Maria ended the call, she leaned back and closed her eyes, trying to will away the throbbing headache. Despite the persistent pain, Maria felt a surge of purpose and excitement. The future held uncertainty, but also tantalizing possibilities. With Raj's unwavering support and the looming potential of a new chapter in the UK, she was on the brink of something extraordinary. As she closed her eyes, the anticipation of what lay ahead danced in her thoughts, leaving her both anxious and exhilarated.

Chapter 73: A Health Scare and Delayed Dreams

A pit of nervous excitement gnawed at Maria's stomach. The interview for her dream job in the UK loomed just a day away, and she was ready to ace it. She'd meticulously prepared her portfolio, practiced her answers, and even ironed her interview outfit twice to ensure it was flawless.

But as the interview day dawned, a familiar ache behind her eyes intensified. It wasn't unusual—stress from the application process and the pressure of the interview itself were often culprits. This time, however, the ache morphed into a throbbing assault, a relentless pulse that burrowed deep into her skull. A wave of nausea washed over her, and as she rushed to the bathroom, the contents of her stomach emptied into the toilet.

Panic gnawed at her. This wasn't just a headache anymore. Worried, she called Regina. Regina, ever the reliable one, immediately arrived at her apartment.

"This doesn't look good, Maria," Regina said, her voice laced with concern. "We need to go to the emergency room."

At the hospital, the doctor's words sent a jolt of fear through her. "Your blood pressure is dangerously high, Maria. 200 over 130! You're lucky Regina brought you in. This could have been very serious."

A wave of gratitude washed over her. She knew her family had a history of hypertension, but she had always dismissed it. Now, the consequences of neglecting her health were staring her right in the face.

The next two days were a blur of tests, medication, and the comforting presence of Regina and Lita by her bedside. Back home, relieved yet shaken, Maria received a barrage of calls. Her family, worried sick, showered her with love and concern. Raj, his voice full of anxiety, offered his support. Adding to the warmth of that support, Dr. Alfonso, a good friend who also happened to work at the same hospital, checked in every now and then, his visits a reassuring reminder that she wasn't alone in this health scare.

Then came the difficult conversation. Raj, his voice gentle yet firm, urged her to reconsider her UK plans. "This year isn't the time, Maria," he said. "Focus on your health. With your blood pressure still unstable, a job search will only add stress."

Maria knew he was right. The dream of joining him in the UK, the meticulously crafted interview plans, all seemed to crumble around her. A wave of disappointment threatened to engulf her, but she forced it down. Her health, she realized, was more important than anything.

With a heavy heart, Maria informed the agency about her plan to postpone the interview and apply next school year. Regina, ever the pragmatist, sighed. "Looks like we're stuck with each other for another year."

Maria offered a weak smile. Another year in North Carolina wasn't what she had planned, but looking at Regina's concerned face, she knew she wouldn't trade their friendship for anything. Her health was on the road to recovery, and Raj's love remained a steady beacon.

The road to her dream might be temporarily blocked, but Maria knew one thing for certain: she wouldn't give up. Once her health was stable, she would pursue her UK aspirations with fierce determination.

Chapter 74: Detour to Delight

Three months had passed since Maria's health scare. The memory still sent shivers down her spine, but thankfully, her health had remained stable. Today, however, a different kind of nervous energy crackled through her veins as she stood at the front of her classroom. It was the day of her cultural exchange program presentation—a chance to share the vibrant tapestry of Filipino culture with her students.

Maria launched into her presentation, her voice clear and confident. PowerPoint slides flashed on the screen, showcasing breathtaking landscapes, mouthwatering cuisine, and the warmth of Filipino hospitality. She shared snippets of Tagalog phrases and played clips of lively folk dances.

The classroom buzzed with interest as students from various backgrounds volunteered to share a piece of their own culture. A lively debate erupted about the best salsa recipe after a presentation on Mexican cuisine, followed by a rhythmic demonstration of the Jamaican dance, "*The Jerk*." There were fascinating insights into Chinese calligraphy and a rousing rendition of the American national anthem.

One particular student, Delphine, from New Orleans, captivated Maria's attention. Delphine's passionate description of Mardi Gras, with its vibrant parades, elaborate costumes, and infectious music, painted a picture unlike anything Maria had experienced before. She spoke of French Quarter charm, the haunting melodies of jazz music, and the mouthwatering flavors of gumbo and beignets.

As the presentations concluded, Maria approached Delphine, her eyes filled with curiosity. "Your presentation was incredible! New Orleans sounds like a truly unique city."

Delphine's eyes sparkled with excitement. "Thank you, Ms. Rodriguez. You absolutely have to visit New Orleans someday! It's bursting with history, vibrant culture, and food that will make you swoon."

A spark ignited in Maria's mind. The disappointment of a postponed UK job application had faded, replaced by a newfound wanderlust. New Orleans, with its vibrant energy and rich cultural tapestry, seemed like the perfect destination for a quick adventure.

Taking a deep breath, Maria proposed, "Actually, I might just do that. How about a weekend trip this coming weekend?"

Delphine's surprise quickly turned to excitement. "Wow, you wouldn't have to wait that long? I can definitely help you plan your itinerary!"

And so, fueled by her student's enthusiasm and her own rekindled spirit, Maria embarked on a whirlwind adventure to New Orleans, a city that promised to be as captivating as its presentation. A detour on the path to the UK can't dim the light of countless exciting possibilities yet to be discovered.

Chapter 75: NOLA

New Orleans, a city pulsating with a vibrant energy unlike any other, unfolded before Maria's eyes. Armed with a guidebook and a heart full of anticipation, she embarked on her two-day whirlwind adventure.

Her first stop was a classic New Orleans experience—a hop-on, hop-off bus tour. As the bus meandered through the French Quarter, with its charming balconies and wrought-iron railings, Maria soaked in the atmosphere. She marveled at the architectural wonders like St. Louis Cathedral, the oldest continuously operating Catholic cathedral in the United States.

Next, she ventured onto the legendary Bourbon Street. The air thrummed with the infectious energy of street performers, jazz music spilling out of open bars, and the aroma of freshly-made beignets wafting from cafes. Although it was a little overwhelming at first, Maria couldn't help but be swept away by the city's infectious spirit.

Hunger pangs urged her towards a local restaurant, where she indulged in a feast of *jambalaya* and *crawfish étouffée*. The explosion of flavors was a revelation, a testament to the unique blend of French and Cajun influences in New Orleans cuisine.

Later, she treated herself to a scenic Mississippi River cruise. The sun dipped below the horizon, painting the sky in a kaleidoscope of colors as the gentle breeze carried the sounds of the city. Maria pulled out her phone, eager to share her experience with loved ones back home.

A video call connected her with her siblings, Lucy and Miguel. Their faces lit up with delight as she virtually showed them around the French Quarter, narrating her adventures in an excited voice. Back in her hotel room, she sent a flurry of photos to Raj, each one a snapshot of the city's charm—a street performer playing a trumpet, a plate of steaming gumbo, the majestic Mississippi River at sunset.

On her last day, she updated her Facebook status—"Living the dream in NOLA! This city is pure magic!"

As she boarded the plane back to North Carolina, a sense of contentment washed over Maria. The trip to New Orleans had been a delightful detour, a reminder that life often takes unexpected turns that can be just as enriching.

Gazing out the window, Maria couldn't help but think about how far she had come. From a little girl dreaming about traveling the world to the woman she had become now, independent, confident, and embracing new experiences. With a silent prayer, Maria thanked God for the life he had given her. She understood that even delays and setbacks could be part of a grander plan. New Orleans had reminded her of the beauty in embracing the unexpected, the joy of exploring new cultures, and the importance of cherishing every moment.

Chapter 76: A Night with Friends

The aroma of sizzling garlic and simmering tomato sauce filled Maria's apartment, a fragrant counterpoint to the evening air wafting through the open window. Regina, Patrice, and Cathy, Maria's closest friends in North Carolina, bustled around the kitchen, their chatter as lively as the sizzling vegetables. Tonight was a night of celebration. Cathy, her face radiating happiness, had announced her pregnancy earlier that week.

As they settled around the table, conversation flowed like the freely poured wine. School memories were shared, punctuated by bursts of laughter. They reminisced about their younger selves, dreams chased and lessons learned. Inevitably, the conversation turned to Maria's life.

The topic of the UK application inevitably came up, stirring a mix of excitement and underlying worry in Maria's eyes. Regina, ever the supportive friend, squeezed her hand. "Don't fret, Maria. Things have a way of working out, even if the path takes a few unexpected turns." Patrice, the practical one, offered a different perspective. "Maybe there's a fantastic opportunity waiting for you in the UK besides teaching. Something that could keep you closer to Raj."

Cathy, her gaze filled with gentle curiosity, brought up the question of marriage and married life. Maria's cheeks flushed a light pink as she spoke about Raj, the warmth in her voice leaving no doubt about the strength of their bond. The distance might be a challenge, but their love, they all agreed, was something to be cherished.

Just then, Maria's phone buzzed, displaying Raj's name on the screen. A collective smile lit up the table as she answered. The conversation flowed easily, Raj's voice a familiar comfort amidst the discussions about life paths and new beginnings. He shared news from his end, laughter bouncing back and forth between them.

With a satisfied sigh, Maria pushed back from the table, her stomach pleasantly full of delicious food and her heart overflowing with the warmth of friendship. The remnants of their laughter still hung in the air, mingling with the enticing aroma of garlic and herbs. Glancing at the mountain of empty plates and the remnants of their lively conversation, a sense of gratitude washed over her.

Across the table, Regina was already clearing away some dishes, a mischievous glint in her eye. "So," she announced, her voice laced with playful challenge, "who's up for some karaoke? I bet I can outsing all of you combined!"

A collective groan arose from Patrice and Cathy, but their faces betrayed their amusement. Maria couldn't help but grin. Maybe the UK dream had hit a temporary roadblock, but tonight, surrounded by the love and support of her friends, it felt like anything was possible.

"Alright Regina," she declared, a playful glint mirroring the one in her friend's eye, "prepare to be dethroned as the karaoke queen!" Laughter erupted once more, the sound a testament to their unwavering bond and their ability to find joy and laughter even amidst life's uncertainties. As the music swelled, and they belted out their favorite tunes, one thing was clear—no matter what challenges lay ahead, their friendship would always be a source of strength and solace.

Chapter 77: A Sea Change

The initial buzz of UK possibilities had quieted into a familiar hum of life back in North Carolina. The anticipation for next year's applications remained, a simmering ember beneath the surface. However, a new urgency had taken root in Maria's heart.

The revelation of the QTS requirement and the subsequent rejection by UK NARIC had been a blow, a sharp right hook that knocked the wind out of her carefully constructed plans. It wasn't a rejection of her dream, not entirely, but a detour, a forced shift in course. The frustration gnawed at her, not from being back in North Carolina, but from the unexpected obstacle—an obstacle the recruitment agency, in their initial zeal, had failed to mention. It felt like navigating a treacherous sea with a faulty map.

The possibility of independent schools without QTS remained, a flickering lifeline. Yet, even that path was shrouded in limitations. Her current visa and English proficiency test wouldn't suffice. Disappointment threatened to engulf her, a heavy cloak that threatened to suffocate the embers of hope.

But Maria was no stranger to adversity. Just as despair threatened to drown her, a memory surfaced—Alice's unwavering support. Her colleague's words echoed in the desolate landscape of her spirit, "Maybe this specific route isn't meant to be right now."

A spark ignited within her, refusing to be extinguished. Perhaps there were other paths, uncharted territories waiting to be explored. With a newfound resolve, Maria embarked on a relentless quest. She delved into the murky waters of alternative avenues, determined to find a way forward.

Days blurred into nights as she delved into the labyrinthine world of teaching qualifications. One acronym after another—SELT, IELTS—became her battle cry. She discovered the International English Language Testing System (IELTS), a potential bridge across the chasm separating her dream from reality. Hope, a flickering flame, began to rekindle within her.

With a surge of determination, she booked the IELTS test in New Jersey. Nights were now filled with a renewed purpose. Textbooks became her companions, online practice tests her opponents in a thrilling intellectual duel. The once-desolate landscape of her spirit bloomed with the determination to conquer this new challenge.

The UK dream might have taken a detour, but Maria, fueled by a potent mix of defiance and optimism, was ready to navigate the uncharted waters. The path ahead might be shrouded in uncertainty, but she would not be deterred. The fire within her, though momentarily dimmed, burned brighter than ever, ready to illuminate the way forward.

Chapter 78: A Leap of Faith, a Spark Ignites

The flickering images on Maria's laptop screen revealed a tapestry of emotions. Her mother beamed a concerned smile, her warmth radiating through the miles. Miguel, her brother, flashed his signature grin, a bright counterpoint to the worry etched on Lucy's face. Lucy, her younger sister, appeared as a nervous bundle, her anxieties a stark mirror to Maria's own. But another face was missing, a constant ache in her heart. The empty space where her father should be felt like a physical void. In the quiet of her New Jersey hotel room, Maria closed her eyes and whispered a silent prayer, "Papa, wherever you are, be with me today. Give me strength."

Stepping out into the crisp morning air, Maria took a deep breath. The imposing brick facade of the IELTS testing center loomed ahead, a stark contrast to the vibrant dreamscapes she envisioned in the UK. While going there might not have been her father's specific dream, she knew he would have fiercely supported her pursuit of any dream that set her heart alight. He'd always encouraged her to chase her passions, and today, she was determined to honor that spirit. With a burning sense of purpose, she approached the testing center, each step a testament to her unwavering determination and the memory of her father's unwavering belief in her.

The Listening Test: The monotonous voice on the headphones droned on, describing a wildlife conservation project in Africa. Memories of countless nature documentaries watched with her father flooded back, each image a silent pep talk. Pencils scratched furiously as she meticulously captured key points and supporting details. When the test ended, a quiet confidence bloomed within her. This was for him, and for her own yearning for a new adventure.

The Reading Test: Time seemed to warp as Maria navigated a labyrinth of passages. One dealt with the advancements in renewable energy sources, another explored the cultural significance of street art. Each passage was a mental sprint, demanding razor-sharp focus and meticulous comprehension. Maria, honed by years of critical reading instilled in her by her father, meticulously dissected each text, highlighting key arguments and evidence.

The Writing Test: The clock ticked relentlessly as Maria tackled the writing tasks. The first, a formal letter, required her to suggest improvements to the local library services. Memories of countless evenings spent with her father in their local library surfaced, a shared love for the written word. The second task demanded a persuasive essay on the importance of fostering creativity in students. Drawing from her own experiences and her father's constant encouragement to explore her artistic side, Maria passionately argued for the benefits of nurturing imagination. Her fingers flew across the keyboard, fueled by a potent mix of grief and determination.

The Speaking Test: The last hurdle loomed large. Face-to-face with a stern but fair examiner, Maria felt a familiar flutter of nerves. However, as the conversation unfolded, the tension eased. The examiner, a woman with a wise smile, asked her about her hobbies, her teaching aspirations, and her impressions of New Jersey. Maria, her vocabulary sharpened by weeks of dedicated study, responded with a newfound confidence, weaving anecdotes and examples into her answers, a subtle tribute to the man who had instilled in her a love for language and learning.

Exhausted but strangely exhilarated, Maria walked out of the testing center. Ten days stretched before her, a purgatory of nail-biting anticipation. Every email notification, every phone buzz, sent a jolt through her. Then, on a seemingly ordinary Tuesday afternoon, while absentmindedly grading quizzes during her lunch break, a notification popped up on her phone. It was the result. Heart pounding, she clicked on the link.

A triumphant grin spread across her face as she read the words: 9 out of 9! Tears welled up in her eyes, a bittersweet mix of grief and overwhelming joy. This wasn't just a score; it was a validation of her relentless efforts, a tribute to her father's memory, and a key that unlocked the door to her dreams. In that sterile classroom, amidst the piles of essays, Maria allowed herself a moment of quiet celebration. A single tear traced a path down her cheek, a silent thank you whispered on the wind, "This one's for you, Papa." The path to the UK remained challenging, but with this victory under her belt, Maria knew she could face anything. The spark of hope had ignited a roaring fire within her, a fire that would guide her every step of the way.

Chapter 79: A Symphony of Relief and Euphoria

The chime of a new email notification sliced through the quiet hum of Maria's apartment, a sound that sent a jolt of nervous anticipation through her. Her gaze darted to the laptop screen, the stark white background a stark contrast to the turmoil churning within her. With a trembling breath, she clicked on the message, her heart hammering a frantic rhythm against her ribs. Each word blurred at the edges as she scrolled down, her mind desperately trying to decipher the formal language. Then, it struck—a single, magnificent sentence that threatened to shatter her carefully constructed dam of emotions.

"We are delighted to offer you the position of..."

A gasp escaped her lips, quickly morphing into a guttural sob. Tears, hot and uncontrolled, spilled from her eyes, blurring the screen as she devoured the remaining words: *"...Maths Teacher at Westbridge Academy."*

London. The name reverberated in her mind, a symphony of relief and euphoria drowning out the background noise of the city. It wasn't a mirage, not a cruel trick of the light. It was a tangible manifestation of a dream that had felt like a distant flicker just months ago. Overwhelmed with a potent cocktail of relief, incredulity, and pure joy, Maria lunged for her phone, her fingers trembling as she dialed a familiar number.

The phone connected with a cheerful ring, and within seconds, a cacophony of excited voices filled the room.

"*Anak*!" Her mother's voice, filled with maternal pride, cut through the joyous chaos. "Did you get the job?"

"Mama," Maria choked out, her voice thick with emotion, the phone clutched tightly to her ear. "I got it! They want me to teach maths in London!"

The news ignited a virtual firestorm. On the other end of the line, Miguel whooped with delight and Lucy let out a joyous cry that could have woken the neighbors. Laughter and well-wishes flowed freely, a testament to the shared journey that had culminated in this euphoric moment.

Maria added Raj to the group chat to inform him about the news. "Raj," she whispered, her voice trembling as a lump formed in her throat. "It's actually happening. I got the job!"

A warm silence fell over the group, punctuated by sniffles and shared tears of joy. In that moment, the distance between them felt insignificant. They could almost feel the waves of happiness radiating through the chat, a testament to the steadfast support that had carried Maria through countless doubts and anxieties.

Esha, Raj's mother, joined the conversation, her voice filled with heartfelt congratulations. "Maria, my dear, I couldn't be happier for you. London will be lucky to have you!"

"Thank you, *Maa*," Maria replied softly.

That evening, Maria, overwhelmed with gratitude, closed her eyes and bowed her head in silent prayer. "Thank you, God," she whispered, her voice thick with emotion. "Thank you, Mama Mary, for your intercession. And thank you, St. Michael, for guiding my steps."

When she opened her eyes, a profound sense of purpose settled upon her. This job offer was more than just a career opportunity; it was the gateway to realizing her dreams, building a future, and being closer to Raj. Ahead lay challenges like visas, logistics, and goodbyes, but in that moment, none of it overshadowed the spark of hope that had ignited an unwavering resolve within her. It blazed brightly, illuminating every step on her path toward a new life in London.

Chapter 80: A Tapestry of Farewells

The South Carolina sun, a warm caress on their faces, cast a golden glow on the reunion on the beach. Maria, Patrice, Cathy, and Regina—their laughter, once a familiar soundtrack to late-night sessions and weekend adventures, now held a bittersweet tinge. Drawn by the allure of celebration and the shadow of goodbyes, they had all decided to travel here for Maria's farewell.

Patrice squeezed Maria's hand. "So, Miss Londoner, how does it feel to be officially on your way?" A playful glint shone in her eyes, but a tremor in her voice betrayed a deeper emotion.

"Honestly," Maria admitted, a lump forming in her throat, "it still feels surreal. Leaving you guys, leaving everything I know..." Her voice trailed off, the vast expanse of the ocean mirroring the vastness of the unknown that awaited her.

Cathy stepped forward. "It won't be forever, Maria. You'll be building a new life, chasing your dreams. And who knows, maybe one day we'll all be sipping tea in some charming London cafe, reminiscing about these crazy Carolina days."

Regina chimed in with a wry smile. "Just make sure you save us some scones, Maria. I hear they're a London specialty, and frankly, I'm willing to risk transatlantic travel for a good scone."

A wistful smile touched Maria's lips. "That would be a dream," she said, her gaze drifting towards the horizon where the sun dipped below the sea, painting the sky in a palette of fiery hues. The vibrant colors mirrored the kaleidoscope of emotions swirling within her—excitement for the new, sadness at leaving the familiar.

As the evening progressed, stories tumbled forth, each one a precious memory woven into the tapestry of their friendship. Laughter mingled with tears, congratulations intertwined with anxieties. Maria received messages filled with well-wishes: a playful jab from her cousin Paula about conquering London fashion, a heartfelt note from Leah and Cora promising frequent video calls, and a message from Christine, brimming with excitement about visiting her in the UK.

News of Maria's departure had also reached her colleagues. The teachers' lounge, usually a haven of lesson plans and coffee breaks, echoed with a chorus of "good luck" and "we'll miss you." They even presented her with a framed photo of the entire faculty, a tangible reminder of the bonds forged during her time there.

A particularly touching moment arrived when Maria informed her program sponsor about her decision to leave. Gratitude choked her voice as she thanked them for the enriching experience.

The most unexpected turn of events came from Cathy. With a shy smile, she clutched a tiny pair of baby shoes. "Maria," she began, her voice trembling slightly, "I know this is a crazy request, but... would you consider being Geo's godmother?"

Tears welled up in Maria's eyes. This wasn't just a farewell; it was a passing of the torch, a promise of a future connection that transcended distance. "Cathy," she choked out, her voice thick with emotion, "yes, of course! It would be an honor."

As the night drew to a close, promises of frequent visits and virtual gatherings filled the air. They stood on the beach, the sand warm beneath their feet, the vast ocean mirroring the vast possibilities that lay before them. In that moment, amidst the bittersweet symphony of goodbyes, Maria knew one thing for certain—the tapestry of their friendship, woven with threads of laughter and tears, love and support, would forever connect them, no matter the distance.

Chapter 81: Across the Pond

The cavernous apartment seemed to echo with the absence of belongings. Suitcases, meticulously packed for a journey across the Atlantic, stood sentinel in the center of the room. Maria, a bittersweet smile playing on her lips, stood before Lita and Danny. Tears welled in Lita's eyes, glistening like tiny diamonds.

"Don't you cry," Maria said, her voice thick with emotion. "England isn't on another planet, you know. You two can visit anytime."

Lita squeezed her tightly, her voice trembling. "It's the distance, darling. It's just..." she trailed off, unable to articulate the depth of the impending separation. "We'll miss you more than words can say."

Danny stepped forward, his goofy grin subdued. "Yeah, those afternoon *meriendas* won't be the same without you."

Maria chuckled, a lump forming in her throat. "Hey, you know me. A video call away. Besides, maybe you can book a flight to London sometime."

Lita swatted him playfully. "Maybe," she conceded, a watery smile breaking through her tears.

Pulling them both into a tight embrace, Maria thanked them for everything. For their unwavering support, the endless laughter, and the memories that would forever be a warm glow in her heart. Saying goodbye was never easy, but amidst the sorrow, a spark of excitement flickered within her. A new chapter awaited, a new life across the ocean, and she couldn't wait to explore everything the UK had in store.

Later that day, Regina, ever the dependable friend, navigated the bustling highway with practiced ease. Patrice and Cathy occupied the back seat, a comfortable silence settling over them. The air crackled with unspoken emotions—the weight of goodbyes intertwined with the anticipation of Maria's new beginnings.

Regina, sensing the mood, cranked up the volume on the car stereo. The opening chords of "*What's Up?*" by 4 Non Blondes filled the car, a song that held a thousand memories of late-night adventures and whispered secrets.

Cathy, her voice thick with unshed tears, belted out the chorus, "What's going on? And why does it feel like this?" A watery smile flickered across Maria's lips. "Because goodbyes suck, Cath," she replied, her voice rough.

The car continued its journey, the music a shared soundtrack to their emotions. They arrived at the airport, the sight triggering a fresh wave of goodbyes. Hugs were exchanged, long and tight, each one a silent promise to stay connected.

Finally, the time came. With one last tearful embrace, Maria shouldered her backpack and walked towards the security checkpoint. The weight of the suitcases wasn't the only heavy thing she carried. There was a bittersweet pang in her chest, a mix of excitement and apprehension for the unknown adventure that awaited her.

As she approached the security line, she cast a final glance back. A lump formed in her throat, but a small smile tugged at the corner of her lips. She raised a hand in a farewell gesture, mouthing a silent "I love you" before disappearing into the bustling crowd.

The security lines were long, a tedious wait punctuated by the cacophony of travelers. But even amidst the airport chaos, Maria couldn't shake the feeling of a new beginning. She scrolled through her phone, looking at photos of quaint English villages and historical landmarks she had bookmarked.

Once onboard the plane, Maria settled into her window seat. Gazing out at the sprawling city shrinking beneath her, a strange sense of peace settled over her. Taking a deep breath, she pulled out her phone and started writing a message to Lita, Danny and her friends. "Just boarded," it read. "Here's to new beginnings!"

Chapter 82: Facebook Post 3

FAITH, HOPE AND LOVE.

These three, the Apostle Paul wrote, but the greatest of these is love. And it was love, in all its fierce and unwavering forms, that had propelled me across the pond. My journey to the UK hadn't been a smooth glide. It had been a gauntlet, a test of my spirit as much as my physical resilience.

My health condition, a constant shadow, had threatened to derail my plans at every turn. Doctor's appointments and medication schedules became unwelcome companions. Then there was the QTS process, a bureaucratic labyrinth that seemed designed to sap even the most determined soul. Countless applications, endless paperwork, and the gnawing anxiety of waiting—it was enough to make anyone lose hope.

But I refused to yield. My faith, a gift from God, remained unshakeable. I prayed to Mama Mary, my guiding light, for strength and solace. I called upon St. Michael, the warrior saint, to shield me from doubt and despair. Their presence, though unseen, was a constant source of comfort.

The unwavering faith of my family was another powerful force. Their voices, a steady source of encouragement across the miles, reminded me of the dreams that my mother and my late father had nurtured together. Lita and Danny, my landlords, bombarded me with pep talks and funny memes to keep my spirits high. Patrice, Regina, and Cathy, my pillars of support, offered a listening ear and practical advice, helping me navigate the UK maze.

Raj's love, a tangible force, became my armor. It fueled my determination to overcome the hurdles, to push through the exhaustion, and to silence the voice of doubt that whispered in my ear. I found solace in Filipino communities, connecting with others facing similar challenges. Their shared experiences and unwavering support became a lifeline, a reminder that I wasn't alone in this fight.

And so, I persevered. I meticulously managed my health and embraced the support that surrounded me. Finally, the day arrived—the day my visa was approved, the day I booked my flight across the Atlantic. It was a day etched in triumph, a testament to the power of faith, hope, and most importantly, love.

Now, as the plane soared towards my new life, a wave of gratitude washed over me. To my family and friends—to everyone who had believed in me when I faltered, and cheered me on when I stumbled—I offered a silent thank you. Your unwavering love had been the wind beneath my wings, propelling me across the pond and into the exciting future that awaited me in the UK.

Looking ahead, I couldn't help but smile. With Raj by my side, a supportive network around me, and a fulfilling career *waiting, I knew this new chapter in the UK would be filled with challenges and triumphs, laughter and love. It was a future I eagerly embraced, forever grateful for the faith, hope, and love that had brought me here.*

Westbridge Academy, here I come!

#ToGodBeTheGlory

Chapter 83: England, United Kingdom

The sterile air of Heathrow Airport couldn't smother the nervous thrumming in Maria's chest. Four years. A thousand texts, countless video calls, and a lifetime of longing condensed into the next few steps. She clutched the worn leather strap of her carry-on, its familiar weight a grounding force amidst the whirlwind of emotions.

Exiting the arrivals hall, she was greeted by the symphony of accents and the bustling energy of a city perpetually in motion. Her eyes darted, searching for the familiar mop of dark hair that had haunted her dreams for far too long.

A wave of hope surged within her, and then, there he was. Raj. Leaner, perhaps, with a hint of worry lines etching his forehead, but unmistakably him. Her Raj.

He stood a little apart from the crowd, a shy smile tugging at the corners of his lips. Time seemed to slow as their eyes met. The years, the miles, the anxieties—they all melted away in that single glance.

With a strangled cry, Maria broke into a run. The polished floor blurred beneath her feet, the din of the airport fading into a distant roar. Raj mirrored her charge, their steps echoing in the vast hall as they closed the distance with a desperate yearning.

He reached her first, his arms wrapping around her like a lifeline. Tears welled up in Maria's eyes, spilling over as she buried her face in the familiar warmth of his chest. The scent of his cologne, a mix of sandalwood and something uniquely him, sent a jolt of pure joy through her.

His hold tightened, a strangled sigh escaping his lips. "Maria," he whispered, his voice thick with emotion.

They held each other for what felt like an eternity, a silent conversation shared through the press of their bodies. The ache of separation, the unwavering love, the unspoken promises—it all flowed between them in a powerful current.

Finally, Raj pulled back a fraction, his gaze roaming over her face. He cupped her cheeks, his thumbs tracing the gentle curve of her jaw. A soft smile bloomed on his face. "You're here," he breathed, disbelief lacing his voice.

Maria nodded, tears glistening on her lashes. "I'm here," she confirmed, her voice hoarse with emotion.

Their eyes met again, a spark of electricity leaping between them. The world around them faded away, leaving only the raw intensity of their connection. There, amidst the chaos of Heathrow Airport, their lips met in a kiss that was as desperate as it was tender.

A kiss that spoke of a love that had endured distance, time, and every doubt. A kiss that whispered a promise of a future, finally, together.

Chapter 84: Together Forever

Maria and Raj had spent an enchanting week exploring London's iconic landmarks. From the architectural marvel of Tower Bridge to the historic grandeur of Westminster Abbey, each sight left them in awe. The modern allure of the London Eye contrasted beautifully with the regal splendor of Buckingham Palace. For Maria, witnessing these world-famous sites firsthand was a dream realized, a testament to her remarkable journey from humble beginnings.

On this crisp spring day, they found themselves hand in hand, strolling through the resplendent gardens of Kensington Palace. The air was alive with the promise of new beginnings, fragrant with blooming flowers painting the landscape in vibrant hues. Maria's eyes sparkled with wonder as they meandered along the winding pathways, drinking in the tranquil beauty surrounding them.

As they reached a secluded spot beneath a canopy of cherry blossoms, Raj paused, turning to face Maria. His eyes, brimming with love and resolve, met hers.

"Maria," he began, his voice steady yet laden with emotion, "Our journey together has been extraordinary. Will you make me the happiest man alive and marry me? Are you ready to explore the rest of the world by my side?"

Maria's heart soared. This moment, long hoped for but never presumed, had arrived. Tears of joy welled in her eyes as she nodded emphatically. "Yes, Raj. Yes, with all my heart!"

With trembling hands, Raj slipped a ring onto her finger—a symbol of their enduring love and shared dreams. They embraced tightly, the beauty of Kensington Gardens bearing witness to the start of their new chapter.

Overwhelmed with joy, Maria reached for her phone, eager to share the news. "Mama," she exclaimed, her voice quivering with excitement, "You won't believe what just happened!"

Simultaneously, Raj called his mother Esha, his voice brimming with pride and elation as he shared their joyous news.

As the chapter draws to a close, Maria and Raj standing hand in hand, gazing out over the serene gardens of Kensington Palace. Their hearts overflow with love and anticipation for the adventures that await. The world stretches before them, a canvas of possibilities, and they know that together, they can overcome any challenge and savor every triumph that lies ahead.

Epilogue

At 39, Maria often found herself reflecting on the incredible journey that had brought her to this moment. Sitting by the window of their cozy London flat, she gazed out at the bustling city below— a vibrant contrast to the quiet, sun-soaked streets of her small hometown in the Philippines where her story began.

From the very beginning, Maria had been a dreamer. As a young girl, she had often stared up at the sky, imagining a world far beyond her island. Her journey, however, didn't start with travel; it began with her passion for teaching. In the Philippines, she had started her career as a teacher, molding young minds in her local community. But Maria always sensed that there was more for her out there. Her heart was filled with wanderlust and her mind brimming with possibilities.

As Maria looked over at Raj, his eyes twinkling with the same enthusiasm that had won her over years ago, she felt a wave of gratitude. They had built a beautiful life together, full of shared dreams and adventures. Their daughter, Anna, was now the vibrant center of their world—a reflection of their love and the promise of a future filled with endless possibilities.

"Mommy, what are you thinking about?" Anna's voice pulled Maria from her reverie. The young girl, with her curious eyes and infectious smile, was the embodiment of Maria's hopes and dreams, a living testament to the journey she had embarked upon so many years ago.

"I was just remembering how far I've come, sweetheart," Maria replied, drawing her daughter close. "From the Philippines to Papua New Guinea, then the US, and now here in England. It's incredible how a young girl from a small town has experienced so much of the world."

Raj joined them at the window, wrapping his arms around Maria and Anna. "And our next adventure is just around the corner," he added with a grin. Their upcoming trip to France and Italy was already filling their home with excitement and anticipation.

As they planned their journey, Maria marveled at how the world had expanded for her, from the narrow streets of her childhood to the sprawling cities and landscapes she had yet to explore. Paris and Rome awaited—a new chapter, new memories to be made, and new stories to tell.

"Are you ready for our next adventure?" Maria asked Anna, who nodded enthusiastically.

"Always, Mommy! I can't wait to see the Eiffel Tower and the Colosseum!"

Raj looked at Maria with a knowing smile. "It's amazing, isn't it? How the dreams you once had for yourself are now dreams you get to share with our daughter."

Maria's heart swelled with pride and joy. "Yes, it is. And I can't wait to see where our journey takes us next."

As they stood there, embracing the present and looking forward to the future, Maria felt a profound sense of fulfillment. Her life had been a journey of dreams realized and new dreams born, each one a stepping stone leading her to this beautiful moment.

With Raj and Anna by her side, Maria knew that no matter where they went, they would face each adventure together, with the same fierce determination and boundless love that had carried her from the quiet streets of her hometown to the vibrant heart of London.

And so, as they prepared for their next voyage, Maria looked forward with hope and excitement, ready to continue exploring the world and all the wonders it had to offer. Her story, like her journey, was far from over. It was just beginning.

In the quiet moments, when Maria gazed at the sky or listened to the laughter of her daughter, she was reminded of her roots and the dreams that had brought her here. And she knew, with unwavering certainty, that the little girl who once dreamed by the window had found her place in the world—a world she would continue to explore with her family by her side.

To God be the glory.